SHOCKS FOR

This Armada book belongs to:

_____

_____

_____

SHOCKS FOR THE CHALET SCHOOL

ELINOR M. BRENT-DYER

Armada

First published in the U.K. by
W. & R. Chambers Ltd., London and Edinburgh.
This edition was first published in Armada in 1971
by Fontana Paperbacks, 14 St. James's Place, London, SW1A 1PS.

This impression 1981

Printed in Great Britain by
Love & Malcomson Ltd.,
Brighton Road, Redhill, Surrey.

CHAPTER I

CABLE FROM AUSTRALIA

" A CABLE, Miss Annersley."
Miss Annersley, Head of the Chalet School,
looked up from the letter she was writing. Her
eyes grew bright and the colour came into her cheeks as
she held out her hand for the sheet of paper. "From
Canada, Rosalie?"

Rosalie Dene, her secretary and an ex-pupil of the
Chalet School, shook her head. "No; from Australia. *I*
thought Canada when Exchange said, 'A cable for the
Chalet School.' But no luck!"

The Head sat back in her chair and read, half to herself:

"Am sending daughter Emerence to you for next four
years Stop Emerence thirteen years and eleven months
needs discipline and has no manners Stop Please correct
faults and help Stop Send all accounts to Victoria Wool
Growers Modern Assurance Company Ltd. Elm St.
London S.W.7 Stop References from Mrs John Mackenzie
of Manly Sydney known to you Stop Emerence leaving
on next plane for England Stop Completely in your hands
Stop From Hope High Leaps Manly nr Sydney N.S.W."

"Well!"

"I feel that way, too," her secretary agreed.

"Mrs. Mackenzie—Oh, Con Stewart, of course. You
remember her, don't you?"

"Of course I do, seeing she had the pleasure of teaching
me history. Her wedding had to be put off once or twice,
I remember, but he came for her at the very beginning of
the war and took her back to Singapore, where he was
something in a bank. What are they doing in Australia
now?"

5

"Jock Mackenzie got promotion early this year and is manager of one of their branches in Sydney. I had a letter from her in June telling me all about it."

"Well, to go back to business. What about this new pupil who seems to be wished on to us without a with-your-leave or by-your-leave?"

"Well, we have room for her, if that's all."

"But it isn't by any means all! I know we have room. This business of Elfie's would give us that, even if we hadn't had such a clear-out here. At the same time, I'm not at all anxious to fill up any vacancy with a pupil who needs discipline and is minus manners. The ordinary new girl is quite enough trouble as a rule, until she settles down, without any fancy touches being added."

"Perhaps she isn't as bad as the cable makes out," Rosalie suggested hopefully.

"My *dear* girl! When a parent writes like that to one—well, cables, then, if you must be so particular!—it generally means that the girl in question is utterly outrageous. *Most* parents seem to think that their offspring are world wonders of the first water."

"Jo doesn't—nor Madame," Miss Dene remarked.

"I wouldn't be so sure of that. I know Jo prides herself on being able to regard her family with a dispassionate eye; but attack the manners or morals of one of her children and I rather think you'd find you'd roused a tigress."

"No; that's not being fair to Jo," Rosalie maintained stoutly. "She really does try to see straight with her children. She once told me that she didn't dare do anything else since her training *now* would make all the difference to them in the future. Jo's the limit in a good many ways; but you must admit that she takes her motherhood very seriously at bottom."

Miss Annersley relaxed and laughed. "You're right, of course."

Rosalie picked up the slip of paper on which she had typed the contents of the cable and glanced through it again. "What had we better do about this?"

"We can't do anything for the moment. I think the best thing will be for you to ring up B.O.A.C. offices and find

6

out when the next plane from Australia is due. Whatever we do decide about this child, someone must meet her."

"I'll go at once." Miss Dene slid down from the corner of the desk on which she had been perching and went to the door leading from the Head's study to the little inner room which was her own cubby-hole.

"Yes; do, dear. We shall know so much then."

While she was gone Miss Annersley read through the cable again slowly and thoughtfully. Then she laid it down and sat with clasped hands flung across the desk, gazing absently out of the open window at the flower garden, where roses still bloomed magnificently and the borders were aglow with tall spikes of gladioli and great clumps of cactus dahlias.

She turned back when her secretary appeared to say that the line was engaged, so Exchange would ring her back as soon as it was clear. She also laid down a packet of letters.

"Here's the post, Miss Annersley. I just brought them straight in. I thought we could go through them until I get that call."

"I can't say I'd mind if there were no post for the rest of the week," Miss Annersley remarked pensively. She made a despairing gesture towards the pile in the 'Unanswered' basket. "I might manage to catch up with that lot if such a thing could happen."

"Isn't there anything *I* can do? After all, I *am* your secretary."

"Not these, my dear. Heaven knows I hand over every single thing I can. But letters from friends and old girls I *must* answer myself. Now let's see what we have here."

"A new parent—and another—and a third—here you are. Deal with them as usual, will you? This is from Peggy Bettany—and this from Daisy Venables. Another parent—from Hilary Burn—I mean Hilary Graves. Oh dear! How we shall miss her!"

"Yes," Rosalie assented. "Hilary always reminds me a good deal of Jo."

"They've got back from their honeymoon and are settling down," Miss Annersley said, after a quick skim-

7

through. "She hopes to come over shortly to see us all. Here's Miss Wilson's—I wonder how she's feeling, in charge of the Swiss branch and with the first term almost on her? However, there isn't time to see now."

"She ought to be all right," Miss Dene said. "After all, she ran the school all that year that you were absent, after the accident."

"I know; but this will be rather different. Oh! Con Stewart's writing! Now, perhaps, we may learn a little more about this Emerence child. No; don't go away, Rosalie. I shall probably need you. Sit down and I'll read it to you in a moment."

"Listen to this!" she exclaimed after a moment.

With her elbows most reprehensibly on the desk and her chin cupped in her hands, Rosalie fixed her eyes on the reader and listened with all her ears to what followed.

"DEAREST HILDA,—I'm glad I'm nowhere near you, for I doubt if I could look you in the face. And yet a lot of it isn't my fault. At the same time, I imagine that if I hadn't waxed so eloquent about the Chalet School, the Hopes—or, rather, Mr Hope—would hardly have thought of sending that young demon of theirs to you.

"First of all, though, I'll give you our own news. We are quite settled down in Manly and like it immensely. I wasn't sorry to leave Singapore as you may imagine; and at least we shan't have to part with the children now. They, by the way, are nearly off their heads with joy. You can't keep Peter and Patrick out of the water and, if she had her own way, Janetta would be with them. However, I don't consider surfing a very safe amusement for a small girl of five, whatever it may be for boys of nine, so Jan has to be satisfied with going in when her father or I are around. All three swim like fish, of course.

"The house is delightful and it really is a blessing to be away from the awful steamy heat Singapore can produce on occasion. Jock is fearfully thrilled with it all, of course. This is promotion with a vengeance! I enclose some snaps of the house and the family and *when* you feel you can

8

fly out here for a month or two, we've a special bedroom waiting for you. Can hospitality go further?

"Well, I suppose I must get on to young Emerence some time, so here goes!

"To start with, did you ever hear such a name? She's called after St. Emerentiana, a friend of little St. Agnes, who was found sobbing for her at the tomb and was stoned to death by some pagans. If you keep her, you'd better put her in St. Agnes' House.

"She is, without exception, the perkiest, most impudent, do-as-I-like youngster I've had the ill-luck to meet and if I thought Jan would turn out like her, I'd pack my only daughter off to you sooner than at once!

"As a matter of fact, she's the result of being brought up by a pair of the maddest cranks on earth. They think that children should 'be allowed to develop along their own lines,' and have never, so far as I can judge, made the slightest attempt to check their daughter's wildest goings-on. They have a summer home next door to us and the first time we met the young lady was when she barged in on us at breakfast time and said, 'Hello! I've come to brekker with you. What have you got?'

"I will say Jock was equal to her—*I* was stunned into silence and he asked who she was and where she came from. She explained and then said, 'I'll spend the day with you. I'm sick of home.'

"Jock informed her that first it was the custom to wait for an invitation and secondly her parents must be asked if we gave her one. With that, he got up, took her arm and marched her home.

"I think she was so startled by this treatment that the wind was taken right out of her sails. Anyway, she made no fuss. Since then, we've got to know them, and honestly, my dear, if I had to live with them I should be raving inside of a week!

"Mrs. Hope favoured me one day recently with her views on bringing up children and actually called me to account for saying, *'No!'* very firmly to Jan when she wanted to go with the boys.

9

" 'Never say "No!" to a child,' she said impressively. 'You prevent its natural development when you do that. Children should grow up as free as birds of the air.'!!!

"Mr. Hope seems to have a little more sense. I fancy he finds his one and only a complete nuisance at times. Anyhow, Miss Emerence has cooked her own goose this time. Three days ago she decided that life was dull and she could do with some excitement. What does she do, but set fire to a little summer-house at the bottom of their garden for the fun of seeing it blaze? There has been next to no rain for weeks now and the result was that she nearly set not only their own place ablaze, but ours and the next-door neighbour on the other side as well! Mercifully, it was got under control in time, but it was a near thing, I can tell you!

"The result is that Emerence is to be packed off to *you* by the first plane that comes handy, he having been much impressed by all I've said about the Chalet School. I heard of this only by chance two days ago, or I'd have written to warn you sooner.

"Goodness knows what you'll make of her; but for any sake tell everyone in authority—prefects as well as Staff— to keep an eye on her—two if they have them to spare!

"Sorry I couldn't do anything about it, but I *am* warning you now that you've got a real handful this time. And remember, she's between thirteen and fourteen; just the age when a schoolgirl is at the wicked worst.

"The only consolation I have is that the school has managed to reform a good many queer characters in its time and I'm hoping that this will prove to be another— reformation, I mean.

"By the way, there *is* another consolation. The Hopes are literally rolling in money so you need have no anxieties on that score. They can afford whatever you choose to charge and are, I believe, quite prepared for enormous bills. Make them stump up for every single breakage of hers. I've never yet been able to make up my mind whether she smashes by accident or from sheer devilment. She generally manages to leave a trail of destruction in her wake—and don't tell me to stop talking in clichés. You're

10

very lucky to have me talking at all. I nearly let it go; but I couldn't quite do that. Only I know you'll all hate me from the bottom of your hearts for the whole of this term, if not longer."

Rosalie was looking dazed.

"Do you really mean we've a young fire-raiser wished on us? *Oh, lord!*"

CHAPTER II

SHOCKS FROM CANADA

AS if one shock were not enough, the three people who always returned to the Chalet School a week or ten days before term began, received another next day.

The Head, the secretary and Matron had plenty to fill up their time in the few peaceful days before the staff and girls arrived.

After long discussion, they decided to cable the ex-history mistress and ask her to send them any more particulars she could discover. A second cable was sent to Mr. Hope to ask him for the name and address of Emerence's guardian in England, for they assumed that the Hopes would appoint someone in that capacity.

"And, if what Mrs. Mackenzie says is true, I pity whoever it is," Rosalie remarked. "Aren't we by way of 'passing the buck' if we send the little wretch to whoever has to be responsible for her?" she demanded.

"Not in the least. Only giving ourselves a breathing-space," Matron pointed out with her usual common sense. "After all, the first one to do any passing is Mr. Hope. He simply gave no one any chance to say, 'No, thank you!' to his young criminal."

Next morning the post came early for once.

"I can't understand it," Miss Annersley said when the

letters had been duly gone through. "We should have had news from Canada last week at latest and no one has honoured us with so much as a postcard. I hope it doesn't mean that something's gone wrong."

"Word may come today," Matron said soothingly. "Anyhow, short of telephoning, we can't do anything."

Rosalie considered. "It's ten past ten now. What time would that be in Toronto? You allow six hours or so, don't you?"

"Well, you certainly can't ring up just yet. Oh dear! Why must Jo go off to Canada at just this time?" the Head sighed, then rose saying, "Matron and I must go over to Carnbach by the eleven ferry. Rosalie, you can take a holiday, only keep near the house in case there's any news. You've worked like a trooper since we came back and this is never an easy term."

"Thank you, Miss Annersley—Oh, would you mind going to Owens' and leaving the list with them? I have it here and they *ought* to know what magazines and papers we take by this time."

"I'll see to it. Give Matey a call, dear. We shall miss the ferry if she doesn't hurry."

"I'm here," Matron's voice said behind them.

Rosalie pulled the car door open and Matron slipped in while the Head took the driver's seat.

"The Abbess is missing Bill," Rosalie thought as she waved goodbye to them. "And we're *all* missing Joey. Weird how it is! Jo's a married lady and a proud mamma of many, and yet, in one sense, she's as much a part of the school as ever she was when she was Head Girl—or a sickening little nuisance of a Middle, for that matter. In *my* opinion, she'll still belong when she's a doddering old woman of ninety-odd, telling her great-great-grandchildren all about her evil doings at school!—Yes? What is it, Megan?"

"Please, Miss Dene, that old ninny of a Griffiths found this at the bottom of his bag so he came back with it," Megan said, tendering a letter with an indescribable sniff of contempt for the unfortunate Griffiths.

Rosalie Dene took it casually and glanced at it. The next

12

moment, she was dancing a silent jig while Megan stared at her in amazement.

"Something we've been waiting for, Megan fach," the secretary explained as she realised her undignified behaviour. "Thanks, muchly. Is the coffee ready yet, do you think?"

She was not going to tell Megan the news, whatever it was, until the Head and Matron had heard, though the letter was addressed to her. Megan was full of curiosity, but could only go and bring the mid-morning coffee while Miss Dene retired to the study and slit open the long-looked-for letter from Canada.

There was only one sheet on which was written in the characteristic script of Jo Maynard, the school's pride, joy and torment, a message that made her old school-fellow give another cry, part thankfulness, part dismay.

"My dear Rosalie," she read, "Break it nicely, kindly and tenderly to everyone concerned that all is well and I have a fourth son. Much love, Jo.

"P.S.—It was such a cold morning that I decided against abandoning him!"

This last sentence reduced Rosalie to helpless giggles, during which Megan arrived with the coffee and the secretary had to pull herself together and say, "Thank you, Megan," very properly.

"Oh, poor old Jo! And she did so want a girl after three boys, one after the other!" she thought. "When was this written? And why on earth didn't they let us know by cable? They *must* have known how anxious we all were."

She looked at her letter again. "Jo must have got tired by the time she reached the end of it," she thought. "That postscript is very wobbly compared with the rest of it. And oh! The young wretch hasn't dated it, so we still don't know when the baby arrived. How like her! What about the postmark?"

She turned over the envelope, but the postmark was smeared and she could make nothing of it. She glanced at her watch, but it was still much too early to ring up Toronto.

"No one will love me if I dig them out yet," she thought

as she folded up the letter and slipped it back into the envelope. "Anyhow, Jo must be all right or she couldn't have written that. The baby must be going on well, too. Poor old Joey! I hope she isn't too badly upset. I wonder what they mean to call the little chap? She might have told me. One or two words more wouldn't have hurt her."

By the time Rosina the runabout came hooting up the drive, Rosalie was bursting with her news.

"Hello, there!" she called excitedly. "Letter from Canada!"

"Letter from Jo. All's well and she has a fourth son."

"A *son?* Is she disappointed?" Miss Annersley demanded.

"Read and you'll see."

The two heads bent eagerly over the screed. Then Miss Annersley glanced at her watch.

"It's—let's see—round about noon in Toronto now. You haven't rung them up yet, I suppose? Then run along and do it now. We must have more news than this!"

"Oh, I shouldn't, you know," said a man's voice at the door. "Wouldn't you all much rather hear about it from me?"

Three shrieks of astonishment arose as the trio swung round to find themselves facing a tall fair man with clear-cut face, at present one vast twinkle of amusement.

"Jack Maynard!" the Head exclaimed. "What does this mean? When did you come? How are Jo and the baby——"

"Hi! Woa! One question at a time, please! Jo is fine—as well as heart could desire. As for the 'baby,' please make it 'Babies'!"

"Babies!" Three jaws dropped at this shock.

"Babies. Why not?"

"But—but—but I've had a note from Jo herself," Rosalie cried loudly, "and she says a fourth *son!*"

"Quite right. Also a fourth daughter."

"Twins!" Miss Annersley ejaculated.

Jack Maynard nodded, a wide, slow grin curling his lips. "Twins it is."

"When did it happen?" Matron demanded.

"Last week—the tenth, to be exact."

"But," Rosalie cried when her breath had returned, "what about this note of Jo's? She distinctly says 'a fourth *son*'!"

"I know. But you see, Jo, as you know, had set her heart on a girl even though the rest of you kept on warning her that it might be a boy. The night before the twins arrived, she wrote that effusion of yours—all except the postscript which she added the moment they would let her. Then she made me promise to mail it without any alteration. When it turned out to be Felix and Felicity——"

"*What?*"

"Felix Nicholas and Felicity Josephine—I insisted on *that* this time!—Jo chose the first."

"I don't know what she's had to grumble about," Matron said severely. "She had *triplets* as a beginning. However, I suppose she didn't want to be behind the rest of the family, and every last one has had twins except herself."

"But why didn't you let us know sooner?" Miss Dene demanded.

"Well, first Jo didn't want you to know till it was well over; and then when we found I must fly over to attend to some business at the San. we decided it could quite well wait until I was here."

"I hope there's nothing badly wrong at the San.," Rosalie said, referring to the great Sanatorium in the Welsh mountains which had been originally established in Austria and then reopened in Britain.

The school and the San. had always been closely linked. The head of it was Sir James Russell, who had married Madge Bettany when she was head of the school. Jack Maynard had been one of his team and had seen Madge's young sister Jo grow from a wicked Middle to a charming girl. But not even marriage, motherhood and authorship had ever prevented Jo from still being one of the moving spirits in the Chalet School.

"I thought Madge and Jo might want to hear about the

15

Swiss Branch," Miss Annersley said. "Well, tell us what the rest of the family think of Jo's twins."

"Oh, thrilled to the last degree. Unless Jo and I keep a firm hand on them I can see those twins being spoilt to death. Look here; what *do* you girls want my advice about?"

This time, Rosalie refused to be deterred. "We've had something unique wished on to us—literally," she said. "We can't do a thing about it, either, so far as I can see."

"What on earth are you talking about? What sort of a thing? New kid, I suppose—what's wrong with her?"

Then Rosalie had her full revenge for the shock he had given them. She replied solemnly, "We've collected a young—er—firebug from Australia. She's flying home and she was practically on her way when they cabled to notify us. Now, Jack Maynard, beat *that* if you can!"

He sat gaping at her for a moment. Finally, he recovered his breath. "You've—collected—a young—*firebug?*" he said with a pause between the words.

"Exactly," the Head told him briskly, "though I shouldn't have used that particular term myself. Rosalie, *must* you use slang?"

Rosalie went pink. "It was the only word I could think of," she said defensively. "I haven't got over the shock of young Emerence myself."

"Is that her name?" Jack gave a whistle.

Miss Annersley nodded. "Emerence Hope. She comes to us through Con Stewart, mainly."

"You'd better tell me the whole yarn."

"So I will after tea. Meantime, I prefer to have my meal in peace, so take your cup and tell us some more about Jo. She's a nice tranquil subject by contrast!"

"And that's something I'll bet Jo has never had said about her in her life before," he said with a twinkle. "You *must* be in a bad way when you can think of Jo as 'a nice, tranquil subject'!"

"Never mind that. Tell us exactly how she is." Matron backed up the Head at this point.

"Oh, she's very fit. She was about all in by the time they reached Toronto, so we had Noel Humphries to see her and he sent her to bed for a fortnight with special diet. She began to pick up after that and she's never looked back. When the twins arrived, there was no trouble at all and they really are fine babies."

"Where is Jo?"

"With the Blue Nuns—same place Madge went for *her* pair."

"And how are Kester and Kevin?" Miss Dene asked.

"Splendid little chaps. Madge says she doesn't know she possesses even one baby, let alone twins. They sleep for the stated periods and in between are chuckling and gurgling all day long. Both can crawl and Kester was trying to stand the other day. By the way, once they do find their feet, I rather fancy Madge will change her tune."

"And Madge herself?"

"Pounds better and years younger! Jo swears she's gone back to what she was during the early days of the school before ever she and Jem were married. I will say, no one would ever think her fortieth birthday was a thing of the past. She doesn't look a day over thirty. As for Jo, the last time I saw her, she looked exactly as she used to look that last year in Tirol."

"And Margot?"

"Fit as a fiddle. So's Charles, by the way. And that moony kid Con seems to be beginning to wake up at last."

"And you really are staying until next spring—all of you?"

"Yes; you'll have to make up your minds to another two terms without Madge and Jo. Apart from anything else, it gives the new building work a chance to dry out properly."

"Yes; there *is* that," Miss Annersley agreed.

"And then Jo's wild to see a real Canadian winter. She's missed the dry, bracing cold of the Alps a good deal more than any of you realised. This year away from England will do her all the good in the world."

"And what about Robin?" Matron asked.

Jack Maynard's face changed. "Robin? Well, she's all right again, thank God! In fact, she's been certified as completely fit."

"Jack," the Head spoke abruptly, "last term Jo hinted that she was going to do something. Is she engaged?"

"No; but she's entering La Sagesse as a postulant after Easter next year."

There was a stunned silence at this news. Robin Humphreys, ward of the Russells and adopted sister of Jo Maynard, had been a pupil at the school from the time she was six. Her mother had died when she was little more than a baby and her father had been killed while mountaineering when she was only thirteen. For years her health had been a constant anxiety, for she had inherited her dead mother's frailty as well as her almost angelic loveliness. She had outgrown the dread tendencies to a great extent, thanks to the care with which she had been guarded. Then when her Oxford course was ended she had insisted on trying to do settlement work. The result had been a severe illness and when she was convalescent, some of the old symptoms showed themselves. She had been sent to Switzerland for some months. Then, in June, she had flown to Toronto to be with the Maynards. In one of her letters, Jo had hinted at a change in the girl's future, but no one had thought of this.

"Is Robin strong enough for it?" Miss Annersley asked at last.

"Yes; and Canada has topped off what Switzerland had begun. Only we're all certain that she should avoid the damp of England as much as possible. She'll be all right in a dry, cold climate like Canada's; but we all agree that living in England is not good for her."

"I see." It was all the Head said then. For one thing, she was too stunned by the shock to have anything more to say.

Rosalie had, though. "Do you mean," she asked blankly, "that we shan't see Rob again?"

"Of course not, you mutt! In any case, she's coming back in March to see everyone before she begins her postulancy. And if you like to go over, you can see her at La Sagesse. It's a teaching Order, you know. In fact, I'm under strict orders from Jo to get your promise to come and spend Christmas with us. Either Jem or I will be flying back to see to the San. and whichever it is will take you back. You'll see plenty of Rob then. We've got a house, you know. We're too many now to crowd into Madge's. Madge and Rob are having the time of their lives getting it ready for Jo to return to when she leaves the Blue Sisters."

"I'd love to come," Rosalie began, "but I couldn't possibly afford to fly. It costs the earth, doesn't it?"

"By no means. Anyhow, we four are giving you the trip for your Christmas present, so you don't have to worry about that. And talking about worry, what's all this rigmarole about a young firebug coming to the school?"

"I'll give you Con Stewart's letter."

He read it through attentively. Then he sat for a moment or two, considering.

"I don't see what you can do but accept the kid for the moment. But you must write to her people and have the whole thing put on a business footing. They can't just send —Emerence?—to any school out of the blue in that style and you can tell 'em so."

"I had thought of that for myself. But, Jack, do you think we ought to take her in any case. She seems a complete danger to me."

"Firing the summer-house may have been an isolated incident and once you get her away from her home influences and in a sane, healthy atmosphere, the chances are that sort of thing will end."

"I hope so. I've been wondering if I hadn't better just cable them and say I can't take the responsibility."

"You'll have to find out first if they've bothered to find a guardian for her in England. If not, you'll have to have her, I'm afraid. You can't leave a child of thirteen to wander loose about a strange country. I should give her a jolly good talking-to when she arrives and tell her that you'll keep her so long as she behaves herself. The first break and you'll ship her back to her loving parents by the earliest plane available. Perhaps that may help to keep her within bounds. Oh, and don't leave any matches lying about!"

"Don't worry. The place is centrally heated throughout

now. Captain Christy had it completed when we found that we couldn't go back to Plas Howell before Christmas, and decided that in that case we'd finish this year on the island and go back next summer holidays.

"Then that should settle it. Warn everyone to keep an eye on her. Probably it was an isolated affair, the result of utter boredom, and she'll settle down in due course. Now tell me what you're doing about new staff and all the rest of the news. Come on! I'm all ears!"

CHAPTER III

ELFIE'S AFFAIRS

"NOW let's see. Are you all here?" Bride Bettany looked over her party with an anxious frown and checked up on them. "Maeve, two Wintertons, Car Soames, Gay Spencer. Right! Form into line and follow me. Mind you don't leave anything behind, for there isn't time to come back for it and you can do your own explaining to the Abbess if you do. It won't be *my* business!"

The other five hurriedly made sure that they had all their belongings and then followed Bride out of the waiting-room at the station of Sheepheys Junction where they had been waiting for the Bristol train.

This was the first time that Bride had ever been in charge. Hitherto, her elder sister Peggy had seen to them. But Peggy had left the original Chalet School last term to spend the final year of her school life at the branch the school was opening in the Bernese Oberland together with most of the girls who had formed the Sixth Form last year.

As a rule, only the Bettanys and the Wintertons caught this train; but Caroline Soames had been spending the last fortnight of the holidays with the Winterton girls, as she was Polly Winterton's great chum. As for Gay Spencer, one of small Maeve's pals at school, she had never gone home at all. A younger brother had started scarlet fever the week before the Chalet School broke up; two days later, the baby sister had followed suit. They had to be quarantined for six weeks and, therefore, Gay could not go home.

So Gay had spent a happy holiday with the Bettanys. The first fortnight had been spent at the Bettanys' queer old house, the Quadrant, perched high on the cliffs of North Devon. A month had then been passed in Ireland and Gay should have gone home after that; but young John had started a mysterious rash, so the two mothers had both decided that it would be better if the little girl returned to the Quadrant and went back to school with the rest.

"It *would* happen like that, just when *I* have to be in charge!" Bride had said with some bitterness. "As if that imp of a Maeve wasn't enough for one person to handle without adding Gay, who's every bit as bad!"

"You're sixteen and a half and Peg was no older when she first took charge of you lot," her mother told her with mock severity.

"Peg had me to help her. I've no one. Polly Winterton means well, but she's a good deal of an ass at the best of times. As for young Maeve and Gay Spencer, they're a complete pain in the neck when they get really going," Bride had retorted with feeling.

Bride said no more, but she thought, just the same. For years she had depended on her elder sister, though Peggy was a bare thirteen months older than she was. But Peggy had been born with a strong motherly instinct which had had plenty of scope, seeing that she, Rix her twin, Bride and their younger brother Jack had been left to their Aunt Madge Russell when Bride herself was only three and the father and mother had had to return to India where Second Twins, as Maeve and her brother Maurice were called in the family, had been born six months later.

Still with that worried look on her face, Bride marshalled her flock safely on the platform.

"Now are you *sure* you've got everything?" she asked. "Night cases—hockey-sticks—rugs—mags and books—

21

brollies—raincoats? Polly, have you the lunch-basket? Well, thank Heaven for that! Here comes the train! Stand back, Maeve and Gay!"

She and Polly hauled the youngest pair back as the express from Penzance came thundering into the station. An obliging porter flung open the door of a carriage and helped to bundle in the two youngest and everyone's possessions. Bride drew a long breath of relief as Lala Winterton clambered up beside her and the porter slammed the door on her. She was even happier when they were safely ensconced in their compartment and Maeve and Gay settled in corner seats. At Bristol they would be met by one of the mistresses on escort duty and her responsibility would be over.

The train arrived on time and they all tumbled out, bearing their various possessions. Bride counted everyone and everything and then began pairing them to go from their own end of the platform to the one from which the Cardiff train would go.

A voice behind her made her jump. "Hello, Bride! Miss Norman is doing escort and she sent me to tell you that there's fifteen minutes before the train goes, but you'd better hurry, all the same."

Bride swung round to face a small, slenderly built girl with big blue eyes in a quaintly triangular face which, together with her short brown waves of hair gave her a kitten-like look.

"Elfie!" she exclaimed. "How are you. Had decent hols? How jolly good of Miss Norman!"

"Yes," agreed the newcomer in rather an odd voice. "Polly, you can take the kids across, can't you? I want a word with Bride."

Polly Winterton, a lanky red-head of sixteen, nodded. "Oh, rather! Come on, you folk! Maeve, come with me and Car, you look after Gay. See you two shortly. Don't miss the train!"

She swept the others off and the two elder girls were left looking at each other.

"Something's wrong, Elf!" Bride said suddenly. "What is it?"

22

Elfie Woodward, one of her oldest and closest friends, nodded and then swallowed hard. "Oh, Bride! I—I'm not coming back to school!"

"What?" Bride stared at her wildly. "Do you mean you've *left* school? But—but—you're only sixteen and a half—just a month or two older than me! And you're going to Chelsea or Bedford when you're through with school and you certainly aren't ready for that yet! Elf, what *do* you mean? You can't possibly leave school yet!"

Elfie gulped again. Then she shook her head and Bride stood gaping at her in anxious silence. Finally, she got control of herself and gave the simple explanation. "I *have* left—had to! Oh, Bride! Marmee died last week and—and there's no one but me to take charge at home."

"Elf! Oh, my dear, how simply ghastly!" Bride grabbed her friend's hand in a warm grasp. "I'm so dreadfully sorry. Can you—can you bear to tell me about it?"

"That's why I came instead of writing. Miss Norman said we were to go to the platform and then we could have all the time there was together. Come on!"

The two girls set off side by side for the Cardiff platform and when they were safely there and could see the bunch of Chalet School girls thronging round Miss Norman, Elfie drew Bride into a quiet corner and told her story briefly.

"Marmee wasn't well when I got home. She was such a queer colour and she couldn't eat and—well, she was really ill. Dad was away, but when he came home, he insisted that she should go to the doctor and *he* sent her to a specialist. He said—he said she'd left it awfully late and she must have an operation practically at once. Only she wasn't fit for it and they had her in hospital for about three weeks, trying to build her up. Then, a week past Sunday, they did operate. She died the next day."

"Oh, Elfie! I'm so desperately sorry!" Bride's voice was warm with sympathy.

"Well, you see how it is," Elfie went on in a hard unnatural tone. "I don't care if she *was* just my stepmother. I never knew my own and she's been just like one to me. I can't leave Dad and her two babies to just any old housekeeper. He's all broken up and—and kind of dazed.

23

And the boys keep *on* asking when she's coming home. I can't possibly leave them—you must see that."

Bride said nothing, but her eyes were very soft as they looked at Elfie. She knew, almost better than anyone else, just what a sacrifice the girl was making. All her life, Elfie's one ambition had been to be a physical-training mistress. She was by no means a clever girl, but she had worked hard and steadily so as to be able to pass into either Chelsea or Bedford. She was a good all-rounder at games and her gymnastic work was excellent. In Guides she had proved that she could handle other girls and teach as well. In making her decision, Elfie was giving up everything for which she had slogged all her schooldays. At the same time, Bride realised dimly that Elfie, being what she was, could have done nothing else.

"What does the Abbess say about it?" she asked.

"She's sorry; but she sees I can't do anything else. I *have* no choice, Bride. It's the only thing to do."

"I suppose so," Bride said doubtfully.

"Of course it is!" Elfie returned hotly. "Geoff's only nine and Peter's seven. How can I possibly leave Dad and two kids like Geoff and Peter with just a housekeeper—even supposing we could get one?"

"Haven't you an aunt or someone who could come?"

"No; Marmee had no brothers or sisters and Dad's only sister lives in Kenya and has four kids of her own. There isn't anyone."

"What does your father say about it?"

"He hasn't said much, but I know it's a great relief to him to know that I'll be at home to run the house."

Bride looked at her in startled admiration. "But *can* you? I mean I'd go ravers if I had to run the Quadrant all on my own."

"Idiot! We live in a little modern house of just eight rooms. It's a very different thing from a huge place like the Quadrant."

"I suppose it is."

"It certainly is. Perhaps you could come and spend half-term with me? Oh, there's Miss Norman waving and it's nearly time for the train to go. They're beginning to shut

24

the doors. You'll have to scram. Goodbye, Bride! Write to me, won't you, and tell me all the news?"

"Of course I will. Goodbye, Elf!"

The two girls kissed each other hurriedly and then Bride caught up her night-case and went flying down the platform to where Miss Norman was beckoning impatiently from the carriage-door. She scrambled in just in time. Bride hung out of the window waving as long as she could see the slight figure left standing on the platform. When they finally rounded a curve, she turned round wishing vehemently that she need not join the others just yet. Miss Norman was standing behind her. Like the rest of the staff she already knew about Elfie, and she also knew what close friends the two girls were.

"There's a seat for you in there," she said, gently pushing Bride into an otherwise empty compartment. "I'll join you later—if there's time. At present, I rather gather from the noise further along that my presence is badly needed."

Bride gave her a look of mute gratitude as she sat down. Miss Norman shut the door behind her and then ran down the corridor to the far end to investigate what sounded like a free-for-all among some of the Middles.

"Bride will pull herself together by the time we reach Cardiff," she thought. "Poor girl! I'm sorry for her. She and Elfie seem to have been chums all their school-life; and it isn't as if she had Peggy here, either. Oh well, she'll be too busy to mope, anyhow. *Well!*" This last aloud as she entered the end compartment. "What is the meaning of all this noise?"

Meanwhile, Bride struggled with the tears which threatened to overwhelm her. The shock had been a big one, coming as it did on top of losing Peggy's help. She was not given to tears as a general rule and she was thankful to Miss Norman for giving her a chance to collect herself before she must face the rest.

"I knew we'd have to part at the end of this year," she thought forlornly as she mopped her eyes. "I'm slated for Welsen and Elf was to have had a year's work to fill in the

25

time till she was old enough for college. It's only come a bit sooner than we expected."

This was poor consolation, but by dint of repeating it to herself, Bride contrived to banish her tears. She sponged her face in the little lavatory at the end of the corridor and then gave it a light dusting of powder. By the time she had finished she looked more like herself, and when Miss Norman finally appeared it was to find her ready to tell the news of the new branch as seen through her sister's eyes.

"Not that Peg could say much about the *school* side of it," Bride admitted. "They don't open till today. But she sent me pages and pages of ravings about the mountains and the chalets and the goats and things like that. I brought them with me to let our lot read them." She stopped here, for she had nearly choked at the sudden remembrance that Elfie would not form one of "our lot"; but she steadied herself almost at once and went on: "I'll let you have them if you'd like to see them."

"Thank you, Bride. I'd like to see them very much," Miss Norman said heartily. Then she changed the subject. "What do you think of the latest additions to the family?"

It was a wise move. In chattering eagerly about her Aunt Jo's newly arrived twins, Bride managed to forget her own troubles for the time being, and by the time they had reached Cardiff she was her usual self.

It all came back when she stood on the platform, but she had little time to think of it. Miss Dene whirled up to her, exclaiming, "Bride Bettany! You're coming back with me in the car. I've been shopping all the morning but left everything to be called for, and I simply must have some help with the parcels. You're to come round with me now and then we'll have tea and be off at once."

"Why—what's happened, Miss Dene?" Bride asked. Normally, Rosalie Dene was hailed as "Aunt" out of school, since she had known the Bettanys from their earliest days.

"A fire at our usual stationery place. They couldn't send our order and I've had to get what I could here and it means taking the whole lot back in the car or we'll be

26

most appallingly short. Our stocks got very low towards the end of last term. It's all right. Miss Norman knew I meant to snaffle you. Come along at once, or we'll never get back tonight."

She hustled the girl off the platform and out of the station and for the next hour or so they were so busy collecting the big parcels and packing them away into the back of the car that Bride forgot all about Elfie. Nor did Rosalie give her any chance to remember during tea. She kept the girl fully occupied in answering her questions about Peggy, the holiday in Ireland and the latest surprise from Canada, and they had run out of Cardiff and its busy environs and were making top speed along the fine highroad before the secretary quietly turned and said, "It's going to be a stiffish term for you, Bride. We all know that. But just remember that Elfie, being what she is, would never have been happy if she had done as she wants and come back."

"I know that," Bride agreed in subdued tones.

"Then don't fret about it."

"No; but Aunt Rosalie, it's all right for Mr. Woodward and the boys, but what about Elfie herself? It's going to ruin her life."

"Rubbish!" Rosalie retorted bracingly. "It's going to do nothing of the kind. This is just until Peter is old enough for boarding-school. Mr. Woodward told Miss Annersley when he wrote that it's only putting things off for a couple of years. Elfie won't be twenty by that time. It won't hurt her to wait."

"But what about the exam? She'll forget all her work," Bride argued.

"Oh, no, she won't. There are excellent night classes in Bristol and as soon as they can get things arranged, Elfie will attend them. She won't miss anything."

"But even if the boys are away at school, there'll be her father to look after."

"Things will probably have straightened out by then. You must remember that it's not a fortnight yet since Mrs. Woodward died. They haven't had time to see clear ahead. No, Bride; I'm sorry Elfie's last year at school has to go

27

missing, but she'll do all the better when it does come to college. You remember that and when you write, don't fill your letters with bemoanings, but keep her up to date with all the school doings and realise that your job is to buck your friend up—not depress her by wailing over what can't be helped. Yes; you think I'm being very hard," she added as she gave a glance at the mutinous face beside her, "but I'm thinking of Elfie just now. Now we must stop talking. I want to concentrate on the road."

CHAPTER IV

A MINOR SURPRISE FOR THE SCHOOL

THE members of the school who had to meet at Cardiff had all been collected by the three escort mistresses and marched into one of the waiting-rooms where they ate their lunch, picnic-fashion. Later they were joined by a few more groups, and at two o'clock were all standing on the platform, waiting for the Swansea train. At Swansea, the big motor coaches which bore them to the coast would be waiting. At Carnbach, the small Welsh port from which they took the ferry to St. Briavel's, they would join up with sundry others who had come by car and then they would be back for a new term—and a term that promised to be different in a good many ways, as Nancy Chester remarked to Loveday Perowne when they were finally settled in their compartment.

"How do you mean?" Loveday asked.

"Oh, Loveday! What an ass you can be!" Nancy retorted. "Have you forgotten what's happened to Special Sixth and ordinary Sixth? Most of them have gone to Switzerland for a last year there and the rest have gone to colleges, hospitals, offices, or what have you. We shall be top form in the school, and that's something that never happened before—or not in my recollection anyhow. Even last year all Special Sixth had been in the Sixth Form, but there aren't any now."

28

Loveday's eyes widened with horror. "Oh, my goodness! I'd forgotten all about that! Do you mean to say that we Upper Fifths have to pitch in and be full-blown prefects on the spur of the moment? What a ghastly idea!"

"Well, you think it over. I know that last year it was very much the same thing, for Peggy Bettany and all that lot hadn't been prefects, either; but, somehow, they all seemed a lot more experienced than our crowd are. Look what a wizard Head Girl Peggy made! And Joan Sandys ran the games splendidly, not to mention Dickie Christy being all you could ask of a Second pree. Of course, the games won't do so badly. We've got Elfie Woodward for them, thank goodness!"

"But we haven't," Loveday said. "She's not coming back."

"*What?*" It was a chorus from the entire octet seated there. Up till then, they had been listening eagerly to Nancy and Loveday but this was a shock.

"Not coming back?" repeated Lesley Pitt, a tall girl with a clever face. "But why on earth isn't she?"

"Her stepmother died these hols and Elfie has to stay at home to look after things there. My Aunt Gwyn lives in the same road and was one of Mrs. Woodward's pals. She wrote to tell me. There are two kid brothers, you see, and they haven't any relations who could take charge, so it means that Elf must do it."

"What awful luck."

They were all silent for a moment until Nancy announced, "By the way, I've another shock for you."

"A shock? How? What sort of a shock?"

"None of the Kinders will be on the island this term *or* next."

"*What?*" The chorus came again.

"The Abbess wrote to Mummy because of Janice and said that they had decided that it would be better for the babies to be on the mainland during the winter months. They had the chance of a big house about two miles out of Carnbach so they've taken it, and the entire Kindergarten is going there with Miss Alton for Head and all their own staff."

"That's something entirely new for the school, isn't it?" Bess Herbert asked.

"Actually, it isn't. Years and years ago," Nancy spoke as if it had happened in the Dark Ages, "when the school was in Tirol, the little ones were always by themselves in another house. Le Petit Chalet, it was called. They had very little to do with the rest of the school in those days."

"How do you know that?" Loveday asked sceptically.

"Auntie Jo told us so. They had Kinders *and* Juniors and I'll tell you who was head of it, too—Miss Norman."

"When did they all join up, then?" Primrose asked with interest.

"That was when they built a third house for the Middles. Then they decided to dedicate each house to a saint. The original school was Ste Thérèse—after Ste Thérèse de Lisieux, you know—and the new house to St. Clare, and Le Petit Chalet to St. Agnes because she is one of the youngest saints."

"What about Our Lady?" demanded a fresh voice, and the girls all turned from Nancy to see a very pretty girl of their own age smiling down at them.

"Rosalind!" Lesley exclaimed. "What on earth are you doing on this train? I thought you always came round by Chester?"

"So I do; but I've been spending the end of the hols with an aunt who lives at Cheltenham. I saw you crowd all get in here—I was on the late side reaching Cardiff, so I thought I'd go into the other coach and wait until we were well away and spring a nice little surprise on you," Rosalind explained with an infectious laugh. "Any room for a little one in here?"

"Of course! Shove up, Nance! Come along, Ros, and sit down."

Rosalind squeezed in between Loveday and Primrose and beamed on them all. "This is fun! And I'll bet Tom and Rosalie and Co. will be wondering what on earth has happened to me," she added. "Why all this ancient history, Nance?"

Nancy explained and was gratified by the amazement of her newest hearer. As it happened, she was the only member of the party to have a sister of Kindergarten age, so it was news all round and she did so love to be first with the titbits, as she had once remarked!

"If you ask me," Primrose observed, "this looks like being a new beginning to the school."

"Tautology!" Lesley retorted smartly. "A beginning usually *is* new."

"All the same," Nancy said seriously, "there will be heaps of changes, you know. For one thing, Burnie's left and she was almost one of the foundation stones."

"Not quite," Loveday replied. "She's only been teaching six years. I wonder what the new P.T. mistress will be like?"

"Goodness knows. Perhaps they've managed to snaffle another old girl. Burnie was, you know."

"So she was. An old girl would be the best bet. She'd know what we expect," remarked Primrose.

What with one thing and another, the grandees of the school had plenty to talk about and the journey to Swansea seemed considerably shorter than usual. Rosalind had to be told about Elfie and then demanded to be told where Bride Bettany was.

"Miss Dene turned up and yanked her off when we got to Cardiff," Nancy said. "I saw them leaving the platform out of the corner of my eye."

Rosalind heaved a sigh of relief. "Well, that's a mercy! I wondered if she'd gone to Switzerland with Peggy."

"I didn't," Primrose returned. "I wondered if they'd got in the wrong train as they did last year. Remember? They had to come back a day late."

"Bride would take jolly good care that didn't happen again," Nancy said. "She'll be going in the car with Miss Dene. I expect we'll find them at school when we arrive there. *We* had to wait for this train, you know, and Miss Dene can drive when she likes."

"Good fun for her!"

"A jolly good job, if you ask me." Loveday said this and they all stared at her.

31

"Why ever?" Bess demanded.

"Well, it won't be much fun for poor old Bride with Peggy gone and now Elfie left in such a hurry. The Heads —Head, I mean—Oh dear! We shan't have Bill this term, either! You're right, Prim! Tautology or no tautology, it *is* a new beginning!" Loveday sat back with a look of consternation.

Luckily for all concerned, they had reached Swansea by this time and in the flurry of scrambling out with all their possessions and then turning to attend to their Juniors, the big girls forgot their troubles for the moment.

Two people were before them. Red-headed Polly Winterton and her chum, Caroline Soames, were arranging their cases and other impedimenta and Primrose at once fastened on them.

"I say, you two, where's Bride off to with Miss Dene?"

"You know as much as we do," Polly retorted. "They went off together and that's all we can tell you. Ask Bride when you see her."

"Curiouser and curiouser!" Loveday observed. "Oh, well, I suppose it's the best we can do. We shan't expire on the rest of the journey because we don't know where Bride is. Come along, you two, and help to form up quietly. It's a good thing for some of those imps that the prees aren't ——" She stopped short in some confusion as she remembered that there *were* no official prefects at present. Then she rallied her forces. "Prim, you go and stand by the ticket collector, will you, and see they hand over their tickets without any fuss. Bess, you and Rosalind hurry on and be at the station entrance to see about their cases and sticks. Off you go! Lesley, will you see to that lot over there while Nance and I attend to this set of the little angels. They'll take the roof off the station if they're left to shriek like this."

"And it's no advertisement for the school, either," Nancy chimed in. "Mary-Lou and Verity-Anne, stop that yelling. Do you *want* to get us a bad name for rowdiness?"

The two Middles thus addressed stopped short in the midst of a fierce argument. Mary-Lou, a sturdy thirteen-year-old, with two fair pigtails dangling one on either side of her face and a pair of very blue eyes, smiled up at the Senior apologetically.

"Oh, sorry," she said. "We forgot. O.K., Verity-Anne, you poop! I'll settle with you later. Pick up your traps and come on. Sorry, Nancy!"

She moved off with Verity-Anne, a tiny girl of her own age, and Nancy was left to grin at Loveday. "It isn't cheek —it's just Mary-Lou!" she observed. "I say! Look at that crowd! The Dawbarns as usual! I *thought* so! Get into line, you kids, and stop making shows of yourselves! Ruth Herbert, what do you think you're doing?" Ruth Herbert, youngest sister of Bess, stopped her mock feinting with her umbrella and looked silly, while Nancy paired her off with Maeve.

The rest of the elder girls were quick to follow the lead given them by Loveday and Co. and in less than five minutes, the long files were moving quietly to the gate, handing over their tickets and then being marched across to the station entrance with Audrey Simpson and Julie Lucy in charge.

The prefects at the Chalet School had a good deal to say in the school's discipline and once the big girls began to take hold, the younger Middles, at any rate, made no bones about obeying them. It was left to a sallow-faced, dark-haired damsel of fourteen to query their authority.

"Oh, help! Are you the new prefects?" she demanded.

Loveday said nothing; but she looked volumes. Luckily, before anyone replied, Miss Slater appeared. "Hurry up, Phil Craven!" she said sharply. "You're last as usual. And don't argue with the Seniors, if you please. They are here to see that you girls behave yourselves if you can't do it without supervision."

Phil said no more but slouched off after the others, a scowl on her face, while the mistress turned to the Seniors and told them to hurry to the coaches.

"You will hear about prefects at Prayers as usual," she said. "In the meantime, you elder girls please take on all prefect duties."

Miss Slater, as senior of all the Staff present, took charge. "Loveday, you and Nancy and Primrose will go

33

into the first coach. The following girls," she raised her voice slightly, "follow them, please."

She read out a list and the girls climbed in in orderly fashion.

Finally all the girls were safely settled and the coaches rolled away while the girls went on with their chatter, rather more subduedly this time, for, in addition to the Seniors, each coach had one mistress in charge.

This particular part of the journey took rather more than two hours and the girls had their tea on the way, finishing up every scrap of food they had brought with them.

It was as she tucked her cup away in her case, that Mary-Lou Trelawney suddenly turned round to speak to her chum, Clem Barrass, who had the seat behind her.

"I say, Clem," she said. "Do you know what? There isn't a single new girl here. *Aren't* there any this term?"

"I'm jolly sure there are," Clem asserted. "This is the term when we *do* scoop them in. They just haven't come with our lot—that's all."

The three Seniors had overheard the query and looked at each other.

"Mary-Lou's quite right," Loveday said in low tones. "I hadn't noticed it before, but there isn't a single new girl in this coach; and I don't believe there was one on the train."

"Rummy! For I know of at least *two* new girls who are coming this term," Nancy replied. "Beth told me that her friend at Oxford has a young sister who was to come to us; and you remember that girl at Red Gables who was their hockey captain?—Someone or other Hughes, I think— well, Red Gables is closing down and she's going to Welsen and the younger kid is coming to us. They live in Cardiff, so she ought to have joined us there, but I didn't see any fresh faces. Did you?"

No one had, but they knew better than to say anything more within earshot of their juniors. They turned to games gossip and discussion of their holidays and this lasted them till, shortly after six, the motor-coaches rolled safely on to the quay at Carnbach where the broad-beamed ferry-boats were waiting for them.

Most of the girls were glad of the chance to stretch their

34

legs by this time, though they had set off from Swansea in sunshine and reached the coast to find a thin, drizzling rain falling. Every one got into her raincoat, pulled its hood over the brown felt hat worn for the journey, and then no one minded the rain in the least except the games enthusiasts, who wondered anxiously if it had been like this all day and if so, what would the playing-fields and netball courts be like? By tradition, the first afternoon of the new term was spent at games so that new girls might find their places in the various teams as soon as possible.

Tom Gay, who had been waiting for them at Carnbach, turned to her friend, Rosalie Way, to remark, "Hope they haven't been having a few days of this on end, or what's going to happen to our practices tomorrow?"

Rosalie's own game was tennis, at which she was a rather more than averagely good performer. Hockey, lacrosse and netball left her cold; but she assumed an anxious expression and replied, "I do hope not!"

Tom, who was not deceived, gave her a friendly grin. "You'd be a lot more upset about it if this was the summer term. Hockey and laxe don't loom very large in your young life."

Rosalie laughed. "No; but they do in yours. I say, Tom," she went on more seriously, "I overheard some of them saying that Elfie Woodward isn't coming back this term. Joan Sandys has left, so who ever will they have for Games pree?"

"I wouldn't know. Elfie was the really one all-rounder we had. Are you sure, Rosalie?"

"Well, that's what I heard Primrose Day saying to Madge Dawson just now."

"Gosh! That's going to be a nuisance!" Tom exclaimed.

"Perhaps they'll choose you."

"Me! Not a hope! I'm a dud at tennis and my hockey's just average."

"But you're the best at cricket and you play laxe jolly well."

"That's not all by a long chalk. Oh, well, we'll know all about it soon."

"Hello, you two!" It was Nancy herself. "I wondered

where you'd got to. "Why didn't I see you on the train?"

"We came by road," Tom explained. "Rosalie's people have been staying at Laugharne farther back along the coast, and I spent the last three weeks of the hols with them. Mr. Way ran us to Carnbach after lunch and gave us tea at the Bunch of Violets. Then he left us to meet you here."

"Oh, I see."

"Where's Bride?" Tom demanded suddenly.

"Miss Dene yanked her off at Cardiff. I expect they came by road.—Oh, *hang* those wretched kids! Just look at them, having a free-for-all!" And Nancy turned and dashed off to the stern where Gay Spencer, Maeve Bettany and the Dawbarns, once more united, were engaged in a free fight to all appearances.

"Little pests!" Tom followed her, seized Prudence and gave her a shake. "Why can't you behave yourselves? Sit down over there and don't move."

"Are *you* one of the new prees?" asked Prudence, who could generally be relied on to belie her name.

"Wait until you reach school. Then you'll know. Meantime, do as you're told—or you can march over to Miss Slater and see what she has to say to you," Tom retorted; which silenced Prudence for the time being.

"Sickening little nuisances!" observed Nancy, rejoining her. "Well, Tom, I suppose all our crowd are Sixth Form this term. I can't say I'm looking forward to it. Top form and having to set a good example—it's a lot too much like work!"

"We've all got to come to it, I suppose," Tom said philosophically.

"Isn't it getting rather foggy?" asked Rosalie coming up.

"The drizzle's certainly thickening a bit," Tom agreed.

"It may turn to fog later, but I don't think it'll be enough to hurt just yet," Nancy said judiciously.

"Where are you going, Tom?"

"Just to see that Annis Lovell is all right. She's been scared of fog ever since last summer," Tom answered over her shoulder as she vanished among the throng to pick on a very dark, gipsyish-looking girl of nearly sixteen whom she joined with the remark, "Filthy weather! Heaven knows what the playing-fields 'ull be like. Bogs, I should think!"

Rosalie turned to Nancy. "That's like Tom. I never thought of Annis and her being afraid of fog."

"It's what you might expect, though," Nancy said. "She was adrift in a fog and she was as close to drowning as one could be."

"Anyhow, we're nearly there!" Rosalie had turned to scan the misty outlines. Now she pointed at a long dark shape that reared itself up out of the water. "We'll be at the landing-stage in five minutes."

"So we shall. Get some of those kids into lines, will you? I must go and gather up my own belongings."

Rosalie looked doubtfully at the chattering Middles near at hand and was thankful when Miss Slater's voice sounded.

"Girls! We are nearly there. Pick up your cases and other luggage and get into line. Someone will be waiting with the big car. Hand over everything as you go past. It's too wet for you to try to carry anything but yourselves up to school. Lines, please!"

The girls hurriedly scuffled into lines and when the ferry-boat had tied up, they marched off her, down the long stage and into the road where, sure enough, the big car was waiting for them with Miss Dene at the wheel and Miss Denny, Miss Lawrence and a stranger ready to take their cases and pack them in.

Once they were rid of their burdens, they were marshalled along the streaming highroad at a brisk pace, and when they turned in at the great gates of twisted ironwork which led to The Big House where the Chalet School was at present, they were warm, breathless, and laughing and ready for the supper that Miss Annersley, after welcoming them in the wide hall, told them would be ready in ten minutes' time. Then she sent them off to get rid of their hats and coats and change their shoes in the various splasheries.

Loveday and the rest of the eldest girls, turned, with

a secret minor thrill into the superior one used by the Sixth. There on the wall, facing them as they entered, was a notice. They pressed forward to read it.

"After Prayers," it ran, "the following girls will please come to the study. Bride Bettany—Nancy Chester—Primrose Day—Bess Herbert—Tom Gay—Lesley Pitt—Loveday Perowne—Anne Webster—Madge Dawson—Julie Lucy—Audrey Simpson—Rosalind Yolland."

CHAPTER V

MISS ANNERSLEY THROWS A FEW BOMBS

THE owners of the names on the list turned and stared at each other, wide-eyed. Some of them guessed what it meant; but one or two of the younger girls felt doubtful.

"It can't be prefects," said Julie Lucy, a strikingly handsome girl who had achieved a double remove at the end of the previous term. "I mean, look at those names. Madge and Ros and I were all Lower Fifth last term, so they certainly wouldn't make *us* prefects when there are people like Enid Young and Rosalie Way and Ruth Wilson left out."

"There are such things as sub-prefects," Primrose mentioned.

"Yes; but even so, that would be just as good for those others as pree-ship. After all, not a single one of us in the two Sixths this year has ever been a school pree—or even a house pree."

Primrose glanced at her. She was not so sure that Julie was right. Rosalie Way was charmingly pretty, but she had very little influence on her fellows. Enid Young was a delicate girl who could be relied on to spend at least a week of each term in San.; Ruth Wilson was inclined to use a bullying manner with her juniors. The elder girl thought to herself that the Head was not very likely to appoint any one of those three.

Tom Gay, after a prolonged stare at the list, turned round. "Well, the best way of finding out what the Head *does* want with us is to change and ooze along to the study. So they hurried to hang up hats and coats and change into the house-shoes they always left at school. There was a good deal of milling round the big mirror above the toilet basins, but at last they were ready. They left the splashery to the remainder of Upper and Lower Sixth and walked in a body down the corridors to the Head's study.

The first person they saw when they entered was Bride Bettany sitting by the fire the Head had had lighted to counteract the gloom of the evening. She herself was seated before a table on which a coffee service and plates of chocolate biscuits gave promise of a little light refreshment during the interview.

"Come along in," she said cheerily as they entered. "I want a talk with you people and I thought we could do it best over coffee. Can you all find seats? Bride, ring the bell for Gwladys, will you, dear?"

Bride rang the bell and Gwladys, one of the maids, presently arrived with the two steaming jugs of coffee and hot milk. Miss Annersley poured out and Bride and Nancy handed cups and biscuits while the rest exchanged news of the holidays with their Head. But when the last girl had been supplied and she had filled her own cup, she came to business.

"I don't think it can be news to you girls that you are our new prefects," she said.

The blank silence that met this statement caused her to pause and look at them. "Well, didn't you realise it?" she demanded. "You knew that all last year's prefects had left and you must have guessed that the new ones would come from you former Fifth Formers."

"I knew that, of course," Primrose acknowledged. "Only, as none of us had had any real experience, I wondered if you'd hold up the appointments for a week or two till you saw how we took hold."

"My dear girl, the school has to go on. We can't stop

because we have lost one set of prefects. We must turn to and choose others to take their place."

"Yes; but usually the subs move up into full prefects and whoever is new to the job is just a sub or a very *junior* prefect," Nancy said. "It isn't often, either, that we have a complete clear-out of all the prees."

"I know." Miss Annersley sat back in her chair and looked at them thoughtfully. "It seems odd, but both last year and this we have had to appoint a complete fresh body. Peggy and the rest had to do exactly what you people have to do now. That is, begin to be prefects straight away."

Tom Gay took up the subject. "Of course, we guessed that some among us must take on the prefect jobs," she said in her funny blunt way. "The thing that really matters at the moment is who is the Head Girl—oh, and who will run the games now Elfie's left."

Bride, sitting quietly in her corner, made a little involuntary movement, but the other girls were looking eagerly at the Head and never noticed it. Miss Annersley gave her a swift glance before she replied to Tom.

"The Head girl," she said slowly, "is Loveday Perowne."

"Me?" gasped Loveday.

"Yes, my dear. There are four of you who qualify for the post, of whom you are one. The others are Bride, Nancy and Primrose. That being the case, we decided to go by age. As you are the eldest, the choice fell on you. I'm sure you will do well and I know the others will all back you up."

"Of course we will!" came from all corners of the room.

Loveday flushed. She was a quiet girl, who, nevertheless, could take hold when necessary. Without being specially friendly with anyone, she was on good terms with most of the set and had proved herself to be both conscientious and reliable in all she set out to do. When the Heads had been discussing the prefect problem before Miss Wilson had departed for the Bernese Oberland, they had found that Loveday exercised a certain influence over the others and this, when taken with her superior age, made her the best choice for the post.

Wanting to give her time to recover, Miss Annersley went on, "Now for the question of Games prefect. If we had been able to keep Elfie, it would have answered itself. But, as I believe most of you know by this time, home troubles have taken her from us. By the way, I hope you girls will manage to write to her fairly frequently. In her way, she has made a big sacrifice and I know it will lighten her burdens considerably if you keep her up to date with all our doings. She said so to me when I went to see them and I promised on your behalf that she should keep up with us.

"Oh, yes; we'll all write," Loveday said quickly.

"Thank you. I knew you would keep my promise. Well; to go back to the games. Apart from Elfie, we have no one who is really all-round there. Too many of you are specialists."

"What are we going to do, then?" Tom asked.

"This year," Miss Annersley spoke slowly, for she had an idea that what she was about to say might not be popular with the girls who were as conservative as most schoolgirls are over such matters, "we propose that a committee of you should run them, with your Chairman to represent you at prefect meetings and in public. She will be known as the Games prefect; she will also have the casting vote if you ever come to loggerheads about anything. In actual fact, however, each of the different games we play will have its own head who will be responsible for making the team-lists and so on, though the prefect will send out all challenges and reply to all you receive."

There was a pause as the girls digested this information. Then Nancy broke the silence.

"How many will there be on the committee?"

"Four—and the Chairman. Here is the list. Bride Bettany will represent the cricket and also be Chairman——"

"Me?" Bride sounded as incredulous as Loveday had done a few minutes before.

41

"Yes—you. Why not?"

"But—but—I'm a bit of a dud at hockey; and my tennis and laxe are only average."

"Wake up, Bride!" The Head began to laugh. "I told you that the Chairman would have heads of all the games she does not play brilliantly herself to attend to the donkey-work. You have to preside over the meetings and attend to the business; but you will represent cricket only and that will be your special job."

Bride had been startled out of her fit of melancholy with a vengeance. "Well, I'll do my best, of course; but don't you think one of the others would manage better?"

"I'll talk that over with you later. At present, try to realise that we are depending on you as Games prefect. Now for the members of your committee. Nancy will represent lacrosse and also be vice-chairman in case you should not be able to take the chair at any time. Audrey Simpson represents hockey; Madge Dawson tennis; Julie Lucy netball. Nancy will be a full-blown prefect, of course, just as you will be; the other three are subs."

"And what about the other posts?" Loveday asked.

"You will vote for those among yourselves as usual," the Head said. "Not for Second prefect, of course. That still remains a Head's appointment. Primrose, we are asking you to take it on this year."

Primrose looked more dazed than delighted at the prospect. The Second prefect at the Chalet School was quite as important a person as the Head Girl, but it meant a good deal of work and not nearly so much of the kudos. However, she pulled herself together and thanked the Head for the honour as prettily as she could.

"I have just one more thing to say on this subject," Miss Annersley said when Primrose had finished. "Apart from Bride—who will have a good deal of work to do—you four will have other prefect jobs to do as well. We have twelve prefects altogether this term—eight full prefects and four subs. We don't want to add to that number if it can be helped, so we have decided to ask you girls to vote the Games Committee members to minor posts."

"Yes, Miss Annersley," they murmured.

"Any more coffee? Pass your cups along. Rosalind, hand the biscuits round, please. Junior Middles are having supper now; but you Seniors won't have yours till after Prayers, so this won't spoil your meal."

She refilled the cups and then proceeded to let off a small bombshell among them.

"I don't know if you have had time to notice that no new girls have come with you today?" she said.

Primrose chuckled. "Mary-Lou Trelawney did," she replied. "She told Clem Barrass about it in loud clear tones and demanded to know if Clem thought we hadn't any this term. Clem assured her that we were sure to—they just didn't happen to have come with our crowd. I don't think we'd thought of it till then, though."

"Clem was quite right. As a matter of fact, we have a rather larger number of new girls than usual—seventeen for St. Agnes, which is the new Kindergarten house about which I will tell you presently, and twenty-two for here. That makes thirty-nine altogether. With all the Seniors leaving, as well as one or two others, we have enough room for more girls. Also, we have made different arrangements for the Kindergarten, First and two Second forms." And she proceeded to explain to them. Then she went on, "Most of them are Middles, as usual; but there are four Seniors as well—one for Upper Fifth, one for Lower Fifth A and two for the B division of Lower Fifth."

"But where are they?" Nancy demanded.

"Not coming until tomorrow." The Head sat back and looked at them. Miss Wilson and I talked it over and also consulted Madame and Joey Maynard, and we all decided that it would be wiser to have all you former pupils on the first day and the new girls on the second, when you will all have had time to settle in. So you won't see any of them till tomorrow at tea-time."

The three people responsible for the winter games exchanged looks of dismay at this. Then Nancy spoke.

"But what are we to do about team practices to find out who wants to play what?" she demanded.

"My dear girl! Your English!" the Head protested. "You will have the whole of Saturday morning and afternoon to see to that. There is no match of course and there will be no walk. I may add that I very much doubt your lighting on any genius in hockey or lacrosse. Quite a number of the new girls are foreigners."

"Foreigners?" Bride exclaimed. "I say! What a thrill! Where do they come from?"

"Ghiselaine St. Amant comes from Brussels and Lesceline Prideaux from Lisieux. Then Marie-Thérèse Dubosc and the two de Vignes are from Paris. Then, I think Bride will remember Arda van der Windt from old Tirol days, don't you, Bride? Well, Arda was married twelve years ago and her two little girls, Lysbet and Grietje, are coming to us. I don't suppose any of those seven know anything about our team games. Winifred Etheridge who will be in Upper Fifth should have come two years ago, but she was hurt in a motor accident and has been on her back for a year and spent the last year in Switzerland. She still has to be careful and will not play games at all till the summer, so she is out of it."

"What about the rest?" Bride asked.

"You must find that out for yourselves. They are mainly Junior Middles, however, so won't be eligible for the school teams."

"Are those all the foreigners, Miss Annersley?" Loveday asked.

"Well, we have also a small girl from Australia, but I hardly think we can count her as a foreigner."

The girls agreed, with laughter.

"Now I've given you quite a good deal of news, so suppose you take your turns and tell me anything else you would like me to know."

Bride, however, had one more question to ask. "Miss Annersley, just one more thing, please. We know there are some new mistresses this term. *Are* any of them Old Girls like Miss Burn and Miss Burnett and Miss Linton?"

Miss Annersley nodded. "*One* is. Our new P.T. mistress is a sister of Miss Burnett's."

"Oh, *no!* What fun! Is it Betty or Peggy?"

"Peggy—though I hope you mean to call her Miss Burnett when you see her," the Head replied drily.

"Oh, of course!" Bride was very red. "Only we were nearly all at school with her and I remember her from Tirol days."

"I know that. All the same, I'm afraid you must try to remember that she is a mistress now and treat her with due respect."

"Isn't she awfully *young* to be teaching?" Primrose asked. "I remember her, too. She can't be much over twenty, even now."

"She isn't. She left Bedford a year ago. All the same, from what I remember of her as a prefect, I fancy you'll find that she's perfectly capable of dealing with even the worst of the Middles. Naturally, you Seniors will back her up in every way."

"Oh, rather!" It came as a chorus. Quite a number of the girls remembered Peggy Burnett and she had been a popular prefect when they had been Junior Middles.

Miss Annersley glanced at her watch. "Now I'm going to turn you people out. You still have to find your own rooms and Matron will be quite pleased if you can tackle your own unpacking this evening. Loveday, when do you want to have Prefects' Meeting?"

"Could we have it tomorrow morning after Elevenses, Miss Annersley? We ought to be nearly finished with the unpacking by that time."

"A very good idea," Miss Annersley agreed cordially. "By the way, we have given you a new prefects' room this year. The old one becomes Head Girl's study and what used to be the Sixth-form room is now the prefects' room. Your form room is in the old Upper Fourth. Bride, I want a word with you before you go, please."

The rest rose and filed out decorously, pausing at the door to make the curtsies that were one of the reminders to those who needed it that the school had begun in Tirol where such courtesies are the rule. When Rosalind Yolland had closed the door behind her, the Head turned to Bride.

"It is just this, Bride. We have given you Elfie's place because we thought it would help you to know that you are carrying on for her. Now run along to the others."

45

"Yes; thank you, Auntie Hilda," Bride murmured. She got herself from the room and made for the nearest splashery to wipe her eyes. Five minutes later, she had run upstairs, intent on finding her room and inwardly resolving that she would do her best to fill Elfie's place, even though school would not be quite the same to her now that her closest friend had left.

CHAPTER VI

ENTER EMERENCE

"NOW are we all here?" Loveday looked round the new prefects' room inquiringly.

"Pat, pat!" Nancy Chester replied with a chuckle. "And here's a marvellous place for our prefects' meeting! Look at the *space!* Peggy and the rest will be green with envy when they hear about it. Mind you give her full details when you write, Bride. Don't spare her anything."

"What do you take me for?" Bride retorted.

"A kind, loving sister who will see to it that Peggy and Co. are kept well up to date with all school news, including our latest—er—amenities."

"Stop yattering, you two?" Tom Gay interrupted. "We're all here, so let's get on with the job. Come on, Julie! Squattez-vous and let's get cracking!"

Julie Lucy grinned as she slid into the seat beside Tom. Loveday took the chair at the head of the table, Bride and Primrose, following the unbroken tradition of the Chalet School prefects, sat one on each side of her and the rest settled themselves around the room. Loveday rapped on the table with the end of her fountain-pen and the meeting came to order and looked very grave and responsible.

The Head Girl stood up and surveyed them all. The Second Prefect opened the Prefects' Minute Book and Loveday after gulping, said rather faintly, "I call on

Primrose to read the minutes of the last meeting." After which she sat down abruptly.

Primrose stood up and read aloud—somewhat throatily —the minutes of the final Prefects' Meeting of the previous term; Loveday solemnly signed them and then there was a moment's pause.

"Well," said the Head Girl, "I suppose the first thing in order is to settle about the various jobs. Here's the list. You all have paper in front of you. Will you please write them down. Hobbies—library—magazine—Staff—Juniors —music—stationery—and this term, there are to be two prefects to see to the art, dommy sci. and geography rooms. The Games Committee are to take it in turns to see to the gym. Are you all ready? Then please put the name of the prefect you think best fitted for each job opposite it. By the way, Primrose, Bride and I aren't eligible for anything but our own jobs. Bride will have a full-time job with games, even if she *has* a committee to help her; and Prim and I will be up to our necks as well. Go ahead!"

The three chief prefects might not be eligible for any but their own special posts, but they had votes like the rest, so for the next twenty minutes, all the twelve were sitting frowning over their lists and trying to make up their minds about the various appointments. Finally, the last list was handed in and while Primrose and Bride acted as tellers, Loveday fished in her case and produced a sheet which looked like a blank time-table form.

"This," she said, waving it at the others, "is the form for ordinary duties like Break and Lights Out and so on. We can't do anything about it until we settle the specials because we must consider the folk who do music and so on. Aren't you finished yet, you two? What an age you're taking!"

"So'd you if you were doing it," Bride informed her. "Everyone seems to have been proposed at least once for everything and it's a case of counting jolly carefully to see who has most."

However, it wasn't quite as bad as that, and ten minutes later the teller managed to produce a list which Loveday proceeded to read out.

"Hobbies—Tom Gay. That suit you, Tom?"

Tom nodded. She had been rather disappointed at being left out of the Games Committee, but when all was said and done, she would very much rather take over Hobbies, especially this term and the next when the school at large would be busy in its spare time, preparing for their annual Sale of Work in aid of the big Sanatorium up in the Welsh Mountains which was so closely connected with the school.

"Just my job," she said cheerfully. Then she looked suddenly anxious. "I say, though, what about the sewing and knitting side of it. I can't do much about *that*, you know."

"I'll help you," Rosalind said. "I'd like to and it really is right up my street. We can divide it—you see to the woodwork and so on and I'll take over knitting and needlework at large. That'll be O.K., won't it, Loveday?"

Loveday nodded. "If you don't mind, it would settle it awfully well. That's that, then. Bess Herbert, you take over the library. You appoint a Sixth Form girl who is not a prefect to take charge of the Juniors, only you have to keep an eye on her, of course."

Bess Herbert looked pleased. She was the only intellectual member of a family of four, and a genuine student. She had been anxious in case she was voted to Hobbies or something else of that kind; but the library was exactly what she liked.

"Magazine—Lesley Pitt."

"O.K.,—but I'd like to consult with you before I put up any notices about it, Loveday. I want to know if we can expect any contributions from Switzerland and so on. However, there's time enough for that later."

"I hadn't thought of that. I expect, though, that the Welsen folk will run their own mag. But some of our own girls will almost certainly send us something for the Chaletian. We'll have to leave it over for the present, I think. Staff prefect—Julie Lucy. Well, why are you looking like that?"

Julie's jaw had dropped conspicuously. "Oh, *lor'!* Why me?"

"Because you got the most votes for it," Loveday

replied. "I'm bound to say," she added with a glance at the page she held, "that you had only three; but everyone else seems to have had only one."

"It isn't anything so very awful," Bride put in. "You see that the Staff get their Elevenses and bring the tray away at the end of Break and do any little jobs they want. But it doesn't amount to a lot. You know yourself they're always very decent about asking for help at any time."

"Oh, well, I suppose it might be worse. O.K., Loveday; I'll take it on."

Loveday nodded and went on. "Juniors' prefect—Anne Webster. I'd like to say," she added, "that this seems to be the only post over which there was no mistake. Anne got eleven votes."

Anne went pink with pleasure. She had guessed this would probably fall to her. She was a motherly girl and it was well known that any Junior in trouble and wanting help or comfort, made a bee-line for Anne if she were anywhere near.

"Music—Madge Dawson. You're lucky too," Loveday added with a smile at Madge. "Miss Lawrence is a complete pet. Last year Mollie Avery had Miss Cochrane and you know what *she* was like! And before her, there was Herr Anserl and *he* nearly drove his prefects to battle, murder and sudden death!"

Madge laughed. "I've heard legends of him," she said. "I never knew him, of course. He'd retired by the time I came to school and he died the next term. But you can't tell me anything about Cocky," she went on feelingly. "She nearly sent me up the wall more than once, with all her sarcasm."

Loveday continued, "Audrey, you're stationery prefect."

"Can do. It's an easy enough job the way it's organised here."

"Nancy and Rosalind take over the outside place; and that's the lot. Divide it up between you, you two."

"Then Ros can have Art room. Herr Laubach doesn't love me and she's always one of his blue-eyed darlings," Nancy said decidedly. "The further away I keep from him,

49

the better I'm pleased—and so, I imagine, is he."

"It's O.K. by me," Rosalind assured her placidly. "Though how you *can* suggest he has any blue-eyed darlings, is more than I can understand. If you ask me, he looks on us as being a necessary evil, since you've got to teach something if you're a teacher."

"That will do!" Loveday said tartly. "You're here to discuss prefect duties: not the Staff and their likes and dislikes."

Nancy gave vent to a chuckle. "Don't be so deadly serious, Loveday. Well, what do we discuss now, anyhow?"

"Supervision duties—walks and prep and——"

Loveday got no further. At that moment, the door was flung open and in bounced a self-possessed young person who stared hard at them.

"Hello, there!" she said in a voice faintly tinged by a cockney accent. "What's this place?"

The big girls all stared at her. She was new; none of them had ever seen her before. She was also a Middle, since she looked about thirteen. She was thin, fair, and pretty in a sharp-featured way. Her straight flaxen hair was cut all round her head in an old-fashioned bob, with a deep fringe over her eyes, and her uniform was superfine as most of them realised. They hardly thought of it just then, though, for they were so flabbergasted by her manner that they were nearly breathless.

She gazed round with an air of complete self-assurance and then advanced into the room, leaving the door wide open behind her.

"Did you want anything?" Loveday asked, recovering herself with an effort.

"Oh, nothing. I only thought I'd look round as there doesn't seem to be anything else to do and there's no one to talk to and I'm bored. I suppose you are the prefects. Mrs. Mackenzie told me about you. You run the school out of lessons more or less, don't you? Keep us younger ones in order and so on." She stopped and suddenly sniggered. "I guess you've got a plateful to keep *me* in order!"

By this time, Primrose and Bride had recovered their wits. "That remains to be seen," the former said gently. "I don't know who Mrs. Mackenzie may be, but if she told you anything about prefects, she'll have told you that most girls prefer to fall into the hands of the Staff rather than get across us."

Bride had been thinking. "Mrs. Mackenzie is Miss Stewart who used to be our history mistress," she said. "She's Con Maynard's godmother, too."

"All this has nothing to do with this child." Loveday took charge again. "I don't know who you are, but please remember that if you want any of us, you knock at the door and wait till you're told to come in. Now run away down to the Junior common room. Someone will be able to see to you there. We're too busy just now."

The young lady deliberately planted herself in an armchair by the empty fireplace. "Carry on and don't mind me. I'm interested," she said calmly.

"What's your name?" Tom asked bluntly, eyeing her at the same time as if she had escaped from the nearest freak show.

"Emerence Anna Elizabeth Hope. What's yours?" demanded the newcomer.

"You'll find out *all* our names in due course," Bride told her sweetly. "I can see that you'll have every reason for doing so. Meantime, didn't you hear Loveday tell you to run away?"

"Of course I did. I'm not deaf."

"Then suppose you do as you're told."

Emerence gave her a look that, for cool impudence, would have been hard to beat. "You don't think I'm going to do what what's-her-name says, do you? You're only schoolgirls like me—a bit bigger and older and uglier, of course," she added with sublime cheek.

Bride glanced at Tom sitting next her. Tom nodded and together they rose to their feet and moved on the young lady who eyed them with sudden wariness. Perhaps she felt slightly alarmed. Certainly, she had not realised when they were sitting down that they were quite so big. Tom stood five foot eleven in her stockinged feet and Bride was only

51

three inches or so less. Standing one on either side of her, looking very trim and businesslike in their skirts and blouses and smartly-knotted ties, they contrived to be somewhat alarming, even to Miss Emerence Hope who was never lacking in impudence.

She had small time for thought. Moving in perfect unison, they lifted her up and set her on her feet.

"Now then," Tom said. "March!"

Emerence dug her toes in. "Shan't!" she said briefly.

"Then we must make you. Pick her up, Bride."

Together they took her and frogmarched her firmly to the open door, through which they shot her neatly so that she was forced to take two or three steps down the corridor while they went in again. Primrose, who had guessed what they meant to do, was standing ready and she slammed the door and locked it.

Not that this move deprived them of Emerence quite so quickly. Judging by what followed, she flung herself at the door, hammering on it with her fists and feet and shrieking insults at the top of her voice.

It could hardly last long, of course. The rest of the girls had been sent out for a walk but quite a number of the Staff were about and so was Matron! She had been busy in the linen-room when she heard the disturbance. She might be verging on her fifties, but she was, as Tom Gay had more than once remarked, "jolly nippy on her pins." Emerence had time for only half-a-dozen yells when the beloved tyrant of the school erupted round the corner, come to find out what such a noise meant.

The listening prefects heard her demand in no uncertain tone, "What is the meaning of this? Stop that babyish nonsense at once and come away from that door! You have no business there."

"I won't—I won't!" screamed Emerence. "I *will* go in! They're nasty horrible *beasts* and——"

The yell that ended this sounded oddly muffled. Bride cautiously turned the key and opened the door a crack, the rest crowding round to see what was happening. They were treated—as many of them as could manage to get a peephole—to the spectacle of Matron, with a swathed and kicking bundle in her arms, stalking down the corridor, extreme indignation in every line of her figure, while from the rug she had flung over Emerence issued more of those muffled howls.

"She'll have Matey over if she kicks like that!" Bride said in a stage whisper. "Should we go and help?"

"Not if you don't want to be eaten without salt," Nancy said. "Here's Miss Slater, anyway. She'll *sort* young what's-her-name!"

Sure enough, Miss Slater uttered an exclamation and took the heaving struggling form into her own strong arms with a sharp shake that reduced the convulsions a little and the group vanished round the corner. The astounded prefects withdrew hurriedly in case anyone came and caught them "snooping" and sat down round the table again.

"Well!" Nancy exclaimed when they were seated again. "What *have* we collected this time? And what have we done to deserve it, anyhow?"

"A young savage from somewhere," Audrey Simpson replied. "Could it be the Australian child, do you think? It certainly isn't French or Belgian. I say, Anne, I'm sorry for you if that's the sort of thing you've got to tackle this term."

"I'm sorry for myself," Anne responded dazedly.

"It's the Australian child all right," Bride said decidedly. "Didn't you hear her talk of Mrs. Mackenzie? She's living in Australia now—New South Wales, I believe."

Loveday spoke curtly. "Well, thanks to her, we've wasted nearly twenty minutes of our time and this duties time-table has to be filled in before we finish. The prefects turned their minds to serious work and Emerence and her introduction to them was forgotten for the time being.

CHAPTER VII

FIRST DAY FOR EMERENCE

WHATEVER happened to Emerence in Matron's room, no one except the two most concerned and Miss Slater knew for some time—the prefects, never. However, it seemed to have subdued her considerably for the time being. When she arrived at Mittagessen, as lunch was called, as a reminder of Tirol, in Matron's custody, she looked uncommonly meek for her and she sat down without a murmur.

The other new girls were not due to arrive until four o'clock, but the air-liner bringing the small Australian arrived at London Airport the day before and she had been sent on to Cardiff in the next plane, thanks to the air-stewardess from Australia who vowed ever after that her first grey hairs came during that journey. Miss Annersley had sent Miss Dene off to meet the plane at Cardiff, where the two had spent the night so that they could catch the early train for Carnbach. Once she had handed over her charge to the Head, she had made a bee-line for the Staff room where her comments on the new girl had been trenchant.

"I only wish I had Con Stewart—I mean Mrs. Mackenzie—here for ten minutes or so! *I'd* tell her what I thought of her for landing us with such a ghastly little horror!"

"But, Rosalie, is she so bad?" Mlle de Lachennais asked anxiously.

"She's the world's worst! Even Betty Wynne-Davies at her worst was not to be compared with her!"

"What?" Miss O'Ryan, the history mistress and an Old Girl of the school, sat up suddenly in the chair in which she had been lounging, and eyed Rosalie as if she had suddenly gone mad. "Talk sense, me dear! Betty Wynne-

Davies was about the worst girl we ever had in this place, and I defy you to produce anything worse!"

"You haven't seen this Emerence child," Rosalie told her with some bitterness. "I foresee a bad time being had by all this term." And with this remark, Rosalie stalked out of the room to her own quarters in a very bad temper indeed.

At lunch, Emerence was remarkably well behaved for the time being. It is true that she fiddled with her food, picking out the more savoury bits and leaving the rest, but the two Fifth Formers on either side of her did not see that it was any of their business to tell her about it. As for Primrose Day, the prefect in charge of the table, she wisely abstained, also.

"We've had one taste of what happens when she's roused. Let's have our meal in peace, at any rate," the Senior reflected as she served the pudding.

After Mittagessen, Miss Annersley called a select trio to her. It consisted of Mary-Lou Trelawney, a power among the younger Middles, and her two friends, Doris Hill and Viola Lucy.

"I want you three girls to take charge of a new girl, Emerence Hope," the Head said. "She had to come earlier than the others, so you must look after her for the present. Emerence, come here, my dear."

Emerence shoved her chair aside with little care for Betsy who was bumped with it, and marched up to the Staff table.

"Well?" she said, standing with her legs slightly apart and her hands shoved down through her girdle.

"These are Mary-Lou Trelawney, Doris Hill and Vi Lucy, who will have charge of you this afternoon," the Head said, seemingly oblivious of the rudeness of her new pupil's address. "You three can take her down with you to watch the team trials. Your own don't take place till tomorrow as the Games Committee want to arrange about the school teams as soon as possible." She turned again to Emerence. "Have you ever played hockey or netball, Emerence?"

"Not me," Emerence returned with her most jaunty air.

This time, the Head did take notice of the impudence. "You should say, 'No, Miss Annersley'," she informed the girl. Emerence opened her mouth to reply to this, but Miss Annersley held up her hand with a steely look that somehow silenced the young lady. "There is no need for you to reply," she said; and Emerence was quelled. The Head turned to the rest of the school to say the old Latin Grace with which meals always ended. Then Mary-Lou touched Emerence on the arm.

"Come along," she said. "You've got to carry your plate and things to the hatch and put your napkin away. Then we rest for half-an-hour and after that we'll all go down to the playing-field or the netball courts and see the fun."

Emerence saw with a good deal of surprise that each girl had picked up her plate, spoon and fork and tumbler and, table by table, they were carrying them to the buttery hatch where the maids were waiting for them. She was sufficiently subdued to follow the example of the rest; but when Mary-Lou and Doris took her off to their common room with Vi just behind and the three began to tug out deck-chairs from the pile in an alcove behind a curtain, she was moved to protest.

"Look here, I don't want to take any rest. I'm not a small kid. I want to see those courts and things that woman talked about and said you were to show me. Come on!"

"If by 'that woman' you mean the Head, I'd say so," Vi Lucy remarked indignantly. "There's no need to be rude about it. Anyhow, it's the rule that we rest for half an hour after Mittagessen so it's no use making a fuss about it."

"Rot! Rules were made to be broken!" Emerence suddenly tried to break through their little ring, but they were too quick for her.

Mary-Lou caught at one arm and held on with all her might while Doris grabbed the other and Vi clutched at her gym girdle.

"Don't be an ass!" Mary-Lou said scornfully. "Rules *aren't* made to be broken—not here, anyhow. You'll only get into the most ghastly row, so what's the good? Come

56

on with me! Vi and Doris, you get four chairs and I'll go and bag our usual parking-ground with her. Stop wriggling, idiot!"

"Honestly," Vi chimed in, "it's no good, Emerence. You'll only get caught by someone and sent back. Surely you don't *want* to start the term with an awful row?"

Emerence stood still and looked at them. She realised that they meant what they said. Besides, both Mary-Lou and Doris were considerably bigger than she was. She decided that perhaps she had better listen to them this time. And then some words of her father's that last night at Manly flashed into her mind.

"Now just you listen to me, Emmy. If you do anything at this school to make them send you back, I'll pick out the strictest French convent I can find for you and send you there. What's more, if it comes to that, you'll stay there for the next five years without a single break. Got that?"

Emerence had "got" it. She knew exactly when he meant what he said and the memory decided matters for the trio. She was blankly ignorant of any language but her own, and the thought of going where she must speak nothing but French all day and every day was enough to daunt her.

Besides, though she would never have owned it at that stage in her career, she had been really frightened at the result of her mad prank. She knew as every Australian child does, just how terrible fire can be and, for once in her life, she had been wholesomely terrified.

Mary-Lou and Co. knew nothing of all this, naturally. They took it for granted that this weird new girl would do as they said when it came to rules. Doris and Vi began to pull out the chairs while Mary-Lou marched Emerence across to the corner where they always staked their claim. When she saw the girl already settled there, Mary-Lou beamed.

"Unpacking finished? Oh, good! Look here, Verity-Anne, this is Emerence Hope from Australia and Miss Annersley said we were to look after her and show her round."

Verity-Anne was clearly the same age as themselves, but she was a tiny creature, with long fair curls tied back from a small face whose miniature features were cut with the delicacy of a cameo. Emerence had never seen anyone so dainty and fragile-looking and when Verity-Anne smiled at her out of gentian-blue eyes and, speaking in a tiny silvery voice that just matched her appearance, said that she hoped Emerence would like England and especially the Chalet School, Emerence went down before her like a ninepin.

"Oh, I—I'm sure I shall," she stammered.

"Here come the others with the chairs," Mary-Lou observed. "Come on, you two! Primrose is looking at us and I can see trouble in her eye."

This was quite enough to make them stir themselves and set the chairs up at top speed. They sat down and Primrose, seeing that they were settled at last, left the room after warning them that though talking was allowed today since the library was not yet open, they must not make a noise.

"What's she mean?" Emerence demanded.

"Exactly what she says," Vi replied. "Once library is opened we read during this time. But it doesn't begin till Monday, so most of us haven't any books and we're allowed to talk quietly."

"Verity-Anne always does do that," Mary-Lou put in with a grin. "She's about the only one of us that *never* gets into a row for being noisy. I say it isn't fair, 'cos she has such a soft voice naturally. It isn't because she's a goody-good, so don't think that!"

"I should think she isn't! None of us is!" Doris said rather indignantly, as if to be extra good was something disgraceful.

"Tell us about Australia, Emerence," Vi suggested.

Mary-Lou shook her head. "We must wait for that. The Abbess meant us to explain things to her, and this is a jolly good chance."

"Have you ever been at school before, Emerence?" Vi asked amiably.

"Not me! I had governesses."

"Governesses!" they exclaimed together. Doris adding, "Oh, poor you!"

Emerence grinned. "None of them lasted very long."

"Why not?" Mary-Lou demanded.

"I saw to that," Emerence informed her.

The four stared at her.

"Weren't your people mad with you?" Vi asked doubtfully.

"No fear! Mother thinks children should be let grow up as they like and Father *did*," Emerence returned.

"I s'pose," Verity-Anne said, "you went on until he got sick of you and that's why they've sent you right away from Australia."

Emerence shook her head until her thick straight crop of hair tossed madly. "No, it was Mrs. Mackenzie. She used to teach here and she raved about the place to all of us. So when—well, when they decided I'd better go to school, they sent me here."

"Well," Mary-Lou said thoughtfully, "I'll give you some advice. Don't try to drive any of the mistresses away here by doing mad things. It just won't work. They'll fire *you* first."

"What did you do that put the lid on?" Doris asked with some curiosity.

"Never you mind!" Somehow, Emerence felt sure that the real truth would horrify Verity-Anne and, although she had no idea why she didn't want her to know, she was quite certain that she didn't.

"Well, we won't," Mary-Lou said with decision. "D'you hear, Doris? You're not to be a poke-nose about it. You *are*, you know," she added cheerfully. "Let's tell Emerence about things, shall we? We've only ten minutes or so left, anyhow."

"O.K.," Vi agreed. "What would you like to know about, Emerence?"

Emerence thought. "I guess you'd better tell me more about the rules," she said resignedly. "Then I'll know where I am."

So they explained such rules as occurred to them and Emerence listened open-mouthed.

"But what a lot of rot it is!" she burst out suddenly. "*Why* shouldn't we talk on the stairs and in the corridors? And why do we have to curtsy to the Head?"

"Manners," Mary-Lou said succinctly. "As for not talking, well, the Head once asked us what we thought would happen if everyone could talk all over the shop. There's hundreds of us—well two or three, anyhow. The row would lift the roof!"

"There's the bell!" cried Doris before Emerence could reply to this. "Come on! We've got to put the chairs away and get our blazers. What shall we watch, Mary-Lou?"

"Netball. That's more fun for us. You see, Emerence, you don't play hockey until you're fourteen nor laxe until you're fifteen; but you can start netball at once if you're ten or over."

"Oh?" Emerence said.

"Come on with those chairs!" said a new voice as a big girl suddenly appeared. "You people yatter too much."

Annis Lovell watched them fold up the chairs and put them away, then she nodded to them and left the room while the quartette bore Emerence off to the splashery to collect blazers. There was no talking, she noticed. Not even that chatterbox, Mary-Lou, said anything until they had left the building and were running in the streams of other girls of all ages and sizes, it seemed to the new girl, across the cobbled courtyard, through the great wooden doors and over the grass of a side-lawn. A dive down a narrow walk between bushes brought them to the wide playing-field where the hockey and lacrosse pitches were already being occupied by the teams and most of the older girls were standing about. Mary-Lou did not pause here, but led the way beyond to where Julie Lucy was waiting with five or six other girls, one of whom was bouncing a big ball up and down. As the four reached them, more of the elder girls arrived, and a mistress who had come with them looked round quickly and blew a whistle.

"All here? You know your places? Then hurry up and take them!"

"That's Miss O'Ryan who takes history," Mary-Lou said. "She's jolly decent: you'll like her."

"Mind you keep moving, brats," remarked one of the big girls who had been in the prefects' room that morning. "There's a real nip in the wind."

Emerence found the game interesting to watch. She had never had a chance of playing team games herself, and had only once been taken to a Test match. It was all new to her and her comments amazed the other four.

They strolled up and down the side of the court and then went over to the hockey-pitch until it was time to go in.

Emerence had enjoyed her afternoon and had lots of questions she wanted to ask about the games. But on the way upstairs, she began to say something and was severely hushed by the other four.

"We *told* you not to talk on the stairs," Mary-Lou said.

"What awful rot!" Emerence began.

"Who's that talking?" came a stern voice from the top.

"It's the new girl, Emerence Hope. She doesn't know the rules very well yet, Bride," Mary-Lou promptly piped up.

"Then hurry up and see that she learns them," Bride retorted. "Quiet, you people down there! There's no need to come up like a herd of wild horses!"

"Which dormy?" Vi asked when they reached the corridor.

Emerence stared round. "It's along here, I think."

Bride had overheard them. "What are the curtains like?" she asked, taking a hand.

Emerence considered. "They have yellow flowers of some kind."

"Try Sunflower—and Daffodil," Bride advised Vi. "It's on this corridor, isn't it?"

"Too right," Emerence replied.

"O.K. It'll be one of those two. Where are you three?" Bride turned to Mary-Lou, Verity-Anne and Doris.

"All in Leafy," Mary-Lou responded. "We go to the next floor, Emerence. Vi's down here, though, so she'll look after you."

"And you three scram or you'll be late," Bride told them. "Vi, you be quick with Emerence. You're in

61

Wallflower yourself, aren't you?"

Emerence was to be in Daffodil which was next door to Wallflower. Vi left her at the door and then raced off to change into the brown velveteen which was regulation wear for the evenings during the two winter terms, after handing her charge over to Clem Barrass who happened to be head of Daffodil. Clem was already changed and took charge of the new girl with her usual competence.

"Here, let me fix that frock," she said when Emerence tried to force her way into it without troubling to undo any of the fastenings first. "You'll bust the whole lot off if you yank at it like that."

Emerence, who at least could never be accused of vanity, grumbled something under her breath, but she stood still while Clem pulled the frock over her head and saw that it was properly fastened.

"Haven't you a brooch?" she asked. "A collar always looks so unfinished if it hasn't something to hold it."

Emerence produced a box of carved ebony and Clem picked out a brooch made of a yellow pansy in enamel with which she secured the collar.

"Now for your hair," she remarked.

"I've brushed it," Emerence protested.

Clem grinned. "Well, *you* may think you've brushed it, but that's a long sight more than Matey will. Hand over your brush and comb and let's see if we get it more like something she'll pass."

Emerence was sufficiently overawed by her encounter that morning to do as she was told. Clem sat her down on a chair and proceeded to brush her thick fair hair until the scalp was tingling and the hair looked a little more as if proper care were given to it.

"There!" Clem said finally. "That looks better. Shove these away, find yourself a clean hanky and come on. There's the bell going for tea and even if the Staff aren't there, the prees are and, on the whole, I'd rather tackle a mistress than a pree."

"Why?" Emerence demanded.

"You'll know soon enough," Clem told her darkly. "Now come on!"

CHAPTER VIII

EMERENCE BREAKS OUT

IT may have been the sheer novelty of the state of things, but the fact remains that, for the first few weeks, Emerence behaved herself remarkably well—for her. It is true that some of the Staff had good cause to complain of the impertinent way she spoke to them, but Miss Annersley contrived to pacify them by reminding them that until she came to the Chalet School, she seemed never to have been subjected to any sort of discipline, so it would take some time to bring her into line. As for the prefects, the memory of that ignominious expulsion from the prefects' room kept her well within bounds where they were concerned. Never in her life had she been treated that way and the hurt to her pride made her resolve not to have to undergo it again.

Perhaps her greatest shield was the watchfulness of Mary-Lou and Co., in whose form she had been placed. They were far enough from being little angels, but they had no mind to have the form disgraced by a new girl. They were unable to do much about the way she spoke to the folk they were accustomed to address with a certain respect, but they contrived to keep her from going too far.

However, even with all this, it was hardly to be expected that such a born imp would reform at once and the Head waited, with more uneasiness than she would have cared to admit to anyone, for the explosion.

It came three weeks after term began. On the Sunday it had started to rain in the afternoon, and rained thereafter almost without a break for the next three days, by which time tempers were growing frayed. The school was accustomed to any amount of fresh air and exercise and when the weather prevented this, the girls were apt to grow irritable.

"Oh, *hang* the weather!" Clem said crossly to herself as

she caught up her towels and made for the bathroom on Wednesday morning.

Pollie Winterton, who had the bath before her, kept her waiting, which did not improve matters, and Carola Johnstone who came after was pounding on the door before she was out of the bath.

Clem stalked back to her cubicle in a bad temper, which was not improved by the discovery that Emerence had elected to consider she had stripped her bed when she had simply tossed the clothes back over the foot and left her pyjamas on the floor in a tangle with her dressing-gown.

As prefect of the dormitory, Clem was responsible for seeing that every cubicle was left in the exact early-morning order that Matron preferred, so Clem chased Emerence down the corridor and told her to come back. Emerence turned back with a grumble that there was always something wrong.

"You've not tossed up the curtains, nor stripped your bed properly," Clem said. "And look at your pyjamas! Hurry up and do it while I finish the rounds."

She left Emerence's cubicle and went to inspect Prudence Dawbarn's, who had a tendency to shirk all dormitory work if she got half a chance. As Clem had expected, her pyjamas were on the floor and the dressing-gown tossed down on the bureau instead of being hung on its peg. The dormitory prefect had to waste three minutes before Prudence sulkily cleared up, muttering to herself about "old maids' fussiness!"

That three minutes was enough for Emerence, who had also got out of bed on the wrong side and was in an even worse temper than Clem.

"I don't see why I should do as Clem Barrass says," she thought. "She's not even a proper prefect. I jolly well won't—and if she doesn't like it as I've done it, she can do it herself. She's a lot too bossy!"

With these reflections, Emerence tiptoed from the room and, once she was outside, went flying down the stairs— and *not* the back stairs which all younger members of the school were supposed to use. To reach them, she had to pass the head of the main staircase and, in her present

64

mood, she decided that it was nothing but fussy nonsense to stop them using the big staircase. She just wasn't going to put up with it!

She promptly went down, two stairs at a time, and was met at the foot by Miss Dene, who came out of the study in time to see the performance.

"Emerence Hope!" she said. "Don't you know the rule about the stairs?"

"Yes; but I'm not taking any notice of it," Emerence told her coolly.

Miss Dene eyed her with a boding look. "Rules are made to be kept. Go to your own staircase—and go up it and then come down again—and quietly," the secretary told her.

"Not me! What d'you take me for?"

Rosalie's eyes flashed at this calm defiance, but she had her temper well under control. She laid a hand on Emerence's shoulder and steered her round in the direction of the school staircase.

"Take your hands off me!" Emerence flung at her.

Rosalie merely tightened her grip. "Are you going to do as you're told without a fuss? Or must I make you?" she asked with a certain awful quietness in her tone that made Emerence quail in spite of herself.

She might have given in, however sulkily, but at that moment a thoroughly angry Clem appeared. That was enough for Emerence. She jolly well wasn't going to let Clem see her knuckle under to anyone!

"You just try it on!" she told Miss Dene with all the impudence she could muster in voice and manner.

Clem's eyes nearly fell out of her head and her mouth opened and shut like a stranded cod's. Miss Dene paid no attention to her, though she saw her; and Clem's presence settled the matter for her, too. Whatever happened, this insolent Middle must be made to do as she was told.

"March!" she said. And there was that in her tone that sent Clem scuttling away as fast as she could go.

Now Miss Dene was slightly-built, very fair and gentle-looking. Emerence had had little doubt that it would be an easy matter to wriggle free from her. When it came to the

C

point, however, she found that she had made a big mistake. Miss Dene's grip was firm and, willy-nilly, she was walked to the foot of the proper staircase down which late-comers were swarming. They stopped short when they saw Miss Dene and her prisoner, but she drew Emerence to one side out of the way and waved them on.

"Hurry up, girls!" she said sharply. "You ought to have been down before this!"

They fled at the note in her voice and when the stair-case was clear, Emerence was propelled to the foot again and ordered up it.

"Shan't!" she said briefly.

Miss Dene gave her a look that Matron herself could hardly have bettered. All she said was, "Very well. You stay here until you do as you're told."

Having defied Miss Dene so far, Emerence was much too proud to give in. She clenched her hands and stood stockstill, saying nothing. Miss Dene watched her for a minute or two. "Oh, very well," she said when it was plain that Emerence had no intention of obeying her. She glanced round and saw Bride Bettany who was passing at the moment. "Oh, Bride! I want you!"

Bride came up to them, giving Emerence a look that boded no good for that young person. "Yes, Miss Dene?"

"Will you go to my office and bring me a stool and the book you will find on the table by the window?"

"Yes, Miss Dene." Bride turned in at the office-door and reappeared with the stool and book.

Miss Dene thanked her, took them from her and set the stool squarely opposite the middle of the staircase. Then, while Bride went off on her own errand, the secre-tary sat down, opened her book and became, to all appear-ance, buried in it. Emerence remained standing at the foot of the stairs. She was determined not to move any further up, whatever happened.

From all round came the sounds of morning practising. Some of the girls went past at intervals.

The bell rang for Frühstück, as the school called break-fast, and there followed the sounds of feet marching steadily down the back corridor to the dining-room. There also came the smell of coffee and bacon and Emerence suddenly realised that she was hungry. She moved a little, eyeing the narrow space on either side of Miss Dene hopefully, and decided with dismal conviction that she hadn't a chance of slipping past. As for Miss Dene, she seemed to be deaf. She turned a page and went on with her reading—or so Emerence thought. Actually, she was watching her prisoner out of the corner of her eye. If the girl tried to dive past her, the chances were that the stool would be upset and Rosalie Dene had no mind to be involved in an undignified spill.

The dining-room being at the back of the house, they could hear nothing until the door opened and the girls came out to troop upstairs and attend to their cubicles. At sight of the pair at the foot of the stairs, the leaders stopped short just as Miss Annersley, who had come round by the other side, also appeared.

"Use the main staircase, girls," she said. "Lead on, Loveday."

Loveday promptly led the long files through the corridor while the Head remained where she was. When the last girl had vanished she came forward and spoke.

"What has happened, Miss Dene?"

Miss Dene explained, adding, "I have told Emerence that she stays here until she chooses to obey me."

"Quite right! But a naughty little girl is no reason why you should be deprived of *your* breakfast. I sent it back to the kitchen with a word to Karen who is keeping it hot for you. She will bring it to you in the dining-room and I will stay with Emerence for the present." She added a word or two in French to this.

Miss Dene nodded. "Yes, certainly. Thank you, Miss Annersley. I won't be long."

"Please don't hurry to the point of indigestion," the Head said, laughing, as she sat down in Miss Dene's place.

Miss Dene smiled as she went to seek her belated meal. She came back twenty minutes later, bearing a glass of milk with her which Miss Annersley took and offered to Emerence.

"Drink that, Emerence," she said gravely.

67

"Don't want it."

"I'm afraid that doesn't matter. I have told you to drink it and you must obey me."

"Shan't!"

Miss Annersley turned to her secretary. "Will you send Matron here, please, Miss Dene."

Matron arrived, looking her grimmest.

"What is this, Miss Annersley? She won't drink her milk? Oh, very well. May I have it?"

She took the milk and advanced on Emerence who was beginning to quake. "Now then, Emerence, either you drink this without any more nonsense or I shall put it into you. Which is it to be?"

Emerence opened her lips to reply, but she got a look that literally appalled her into silence. She took the milk and drank it without more ado. Matron removed the glass and herself, while Miss Dene, who had armed herself with some knitting, sat down again.

People going past stared curiously at them, but no one spoke. Emerence felt better since she had had that glass of creamy milk. If she had dared, she would have made a bolt for it—but not upstairs, which lay open to her. She had been told to go and had said she wouldn't and that settled that so far as she was concerned.

The girls went for their morning walk. They came back, changed their shoes and went to their form-rooms. The bell rang for Prayers and, after an interval, the school came streaming back to the form-rooms again and work for the day started. Still Miss Dene had not spoken and Emerence was growing very tired of standing there.

"Please—can I—sit down?" she asked at last, startling herself by the question, for she had determined not to speak if she could help it.

"Yes, you may. Sit down where you are—unless you are prepared to give up this silly defiance and do as you're told," she said. "Why don't you, Emerence? It's so absurd to keep yourself there when just by being obedient, you could go and join the others."

Emerence flushed but said nothing. She sat down on the stairs and the long morning began. Miss Dene finished

one sleeve of her jumper and cast on the other. The first
lesson had ended; so had the second. Break came and went
and still Emerence seemed no more prepared to give in
than she had ever been.

The maids, forced to go round by the main staircase,
eyed her with deep dislike as they went past. They were
busy enough without having so many extra steps added
to their work. The school at large took no apparent notice
of the pair, though Mary-Lou, going to the Staff room on
an errand, gave Emerence an exceedingly chilly look which
made that young woman redden again.

Then Miss Stephens, the geography mistress, arrived to
relieve Miss Dene who went off to attend to the morning's
post, which had been neglected all this time. Miss Stephens
had brought a folding-desk with her. She set it up and sat
marking Upper Fifth's work without saying a word to the
young rebel on the stairs.

When the bell rang for the end of the lesson, her place
was taken by Mlle de Lachennais, who sat preparing
sewing for Emerence's own form until the end of morning
school, by which time Emerence knew that she must stay
where she was until she *did* choose to yield. What
impressed her most about this novel treatment was the fact
that no one had scolded her. On the few occasions when
she had roused her mother, she had been sharply scolded.
She could remember one occasion when she had been
shaken until she hardly knew which end was uppermost.
Mrs. Hope was not always consistent in her dealings with
her only child, whatever she might preach to other
mothers. But here there had been no real scolding and
certainly no one had attempted to shake her. It had been
just this silent waiting until she did as she was told.

"I b'lieve," she thought, "that they'll keep me here
all day if I don't do as Miss Dene said. Oh, but I *can't*!
I just can't give in when I've said I won't."

She sat playing with her girdle. A sudden thought struck
her. They had netball that afternoon and if she didn't give
in, then she must miss it—and she did so love it!

"I can't—I just can't miss it!" she thought wildly. "Oh,

what shall I do?—She had forgotten that it was raining hard.

Miss Dene came along at that moment and Mlle gathered up her work and departed. Emerence could hear the girls in the splasheries. Then the gong sounded for Mittagessen. Miss Dene had brought her little portable typewriter and was typing rapidly. She paid no heed to the gong, but worked on steadily. The girls could be heard going to the dining-room. Then the door shut.

Miss Dene was considering the wording of a sentence when a meek voice asked, "Please—please may I go and wash?"

Rosalie Dene looked up. "Yes; I'll take you to the splashery. Come along!"

She stood up, but Emerence remained crouching on the stairs. Her head suddenly went down on her arm and she began to cry.

"I'm t-tired of s-sitting he-ere!" she sobbed.

"Well, you know what to do if you want to stop," Miss Dene reminded her. Then she added in more kindly tones, "What a silly girl you are, Emerence! Here you've wasted an entire morning just because first you deliberately break a rule and then refuse to submit to authority. Come, stop crying and go quietly up and down the stairs and we'll say no more about it."

"N-no one ever t-treated me like th-this b-before!" wept Emerence.

"I hope you will see to it that no one ever needs to treat you like this again," the secretary retorted bracingly. She stooped and lifted the child to her feet. "Now then, off you go! Be quick and you won't be so very late for Mittagessen."

Emerence was conquered for the time being. Slowly she climbed the stairs, mopping her eyes as she went. Then she came down again, still gulping, but feeling better. Miss Dene had closed her typewriter and folded up the desk.

"Run along to the splashery," she said, "and give your face a good sluice. You'll feel all right then. Mind you go straight to the dining-room."

And that was the end of it. At least, it was all from

Miss Dene who never again referred to the matter in any way. Emerence still had to face Clem, who told her what she thought of her in no uncertain tone. Matron also had a few words to say on the subject of her babyish behaviour over the milk. Matron implied that such behaviour was beneath the youngest of the St. Agnes' Juniors, and further told her that if such a thing occurred again she would be sent to St. Agnes' for a week.

Emerence guessed that if such a thing did happen, her own crowd would never let her forget it, so she inwardly vowed to do nothing to bring it about. As it was, the Head had strictly forbidden any remarks to her or at her about the morning's performance, so, much to her surprise, she heard nothing about it from her own form.

Finally, at six o'clock she had to go to Miss Annersley, who impressed on her that rules were made to be kept and that there was a good reason for every rule.

Emerence was feeling herself again by this time. "But *why* can't we use the front stairs?" she demanded.

"First," Miss Annersley said, looking at her seriously, "because in most cases, it is out of your way. Secondly, because the front stairs are carpeted and if you girls were for ever running up and down them, I'm afraid there would soon be no carpets left. Lastly, those stairs come down into the main hall. We couldn't have girls running all over when visitors were coming. So you see for all reasons it is wiser to keep you to the back stairs."

Emerence nodded thoughtfully. "I see. But why didn't Miss Dene tell me all that instead of making me stay there the whole morning?" she added.

"Because you were rude and defiant and flatly disobeyed her. No mistress worth her salt would put up with that sort of thing. Orders are orders, Emerence, and you must obey them. If you don't there will always be punishment—for deliberate disobedience, I mean. In future, though, if you can't see the reason for a rule find someone to explain it to you before you decide to break it. But if you take the trouble to think it out for yourself, you ought to be able to find the reason without that. Now you may go back to your prep. Please don't be so silly again."

Emerence trailed to the door and bobbed the curtsy it had taken all this time to impress on her was a definite 'must.' "I'll do it—if I can remember," she said.

Then she sidled out and Miss Annersley was left to laugh over that last speech and think it would be a nice little story to add to her letter to Jo.

"At the same time," she reflected as she took out the letter and set to work, "though I'm sure the young monkey is far enough from being a reformed character, I have an idea that this morning's lesson is quite a big step in that direction for her. Anyhow, I imagine she won't be in a hurry to pass her morning on the stairs again!"

CHAPTER IX

MISS BURNETT CREATES A SENSATION

"WELL, I don't know what the rest of you think, but I'm going to start in and clear this bed almost *completely*!" Thus Mary-Lou as she stood gazing over the big garden bed which belonged to Lower Fourth and which looked, as Loveday had remarked only that morning, "a perfect hurrah's nest!"

"Yes, it's pretty bad, isn't it?" Vi agreed, coming to stand beside her. "Loveday was nastyish about it, but you know I don't really blame her. When you come to look at it, it really *is*!"

Verity-Anne stared dismally at the wilderness. "I always thought weeds didn't grow in winter and autumn."

"If you ask me, they grow all the year round," Mary-Lou grumbled. "Just look at all that awful groundsel! And we cleared the bed of it the day before the rain began."

"Yes; but think of the days and *days* of rain we've had since," Lesley Malcolm added. "A week all but a day, isn't it? The way the stuff grows it's had oceans of time to come up again."

"Well," Doris Hill observed, "we'd better do something

about it and do it pronto, or Loveday will have the faces off us."

" 'Ware prees!" Vi warned her with a quick glance round. "You know what Peggy Bettany said to Norah Fitzgerald last term about saying that."

"I know; but Peggy isn't here any more; and anyway, it isn't what you could really call *slang*—not real slang!" Lesley finished with a naughty chuckle.

"The prees think anything expressive is slang," Mary-Lou replied, speaking from bitter experience. "Well, it's no good standing here yattering. *That* won't buy the baby a new hat! Anyone got the spuds and rakes and things?"

The gardening tools were all there and Mary-Lou, who generally ran their gang, proceeded to deal them out.

"Ruth and Priscilla and—let's see—oh, you, Lesley, and Vi and Gwen take the spuds. We mustn't dig up the roots and bulbs and things like that and you *do* know a weed when you see it. June, you and—and Kitty and Catriona and Emerence can have the rakes and rake the weeds into heaps as the others get them up. Verity-Anne, we shall want the barrows to cart them to the bonfire. You take charge of that job, will you. Take three or four other folk 'cos those barrows are heavy when they're full and it'll take two people to a barrow. Ghiselaine, you go with them. You don't seem to know a dandelion from a—a turnip-top!"

As Ghiselaine had spent her life in an appartement in Brussels and had never done any gardening until she came to school, this was true. She was a shy, quiet little person, with enormous dark eyes that all too soon swam with tears, though her friends were doing their conscientious best to train her out of "Being a wet sponge," as Mary-Lou described it.

"What are *you* going to do—besides giving orders?" demanded Peggy Harper, a harum-scarum who occasionally rebelled against Mary-Lou's leadership, though the pair were good enough friends.

Mary-Lou indicated a tangle of roses in the middle of the bed that were rapidly going to briar. "I'm going to cut those right down. I was talking to our old gardener, Preece,

73

in the hols, and he said you should always get your worst enemy to do that 'cos most folk were too tender with their roses to do them properly. I'm going to do them properly. Clem showed me how last Easter."

"How can you?" Vi demanded. "You know Evvy said we weren't to have the secateurs 'cos we might cut ourselves."

"I'm not using 'em, either. I bagged Mother's old cutting-out scissors before we came back. Matey never saw them and I brought them down from my hat-box this morning. They're gorgeously sharp. I got Preece to sharpen them for me and I'll soon have *that* lot cleared away." Mary-Lou was fumbling at the waist of the blue jean overalls she, like all the rest, wore. Finally, she tugged out an enormous pair of cutting-out shears, tied round her waist with elastic. "That's the beauty of overalls. You can hang things down under them and no one ever sees."

Half the crowd burst into peals of laughter. Verity-Anne, however, turned quite pale. "Oh, Mary-Lou! Supposing you'd slipped and fallen? You might have dug them right into your tummy!"

"Not me! I tied up the blades with string, just in case. And anyhow, *I* don't go falling around. I'm not a baby," Mary-Lou said serenely as she undid the twine twisted round the blades and threw it into a nearby bush of flowering currant.

"Now don't start, you two!" Lesley said hurriedly. "Burnie said she'd be along as soon as she'd got the rest started and if we haven't something to show her, you know what she'll say!"

So they turned their attention to their work. Those who had been allotted tools, seized on them and, while Vi took charge of the spudding-up squad, Verity-Anne picked out the girls she wanted in her gang and Gwen Davies marshalled the rakers to one side and gave out the rakes.

It was Four B's turn in the garden today and Miss Burnett had sent them out to begin while she arranged for the other Middles. After that, she had promised to come and see what the form was doing. If they had nothing to show for their time, it would mean a prim walk next week

74

and no one wanted that if she could garden instead.

"What are *we* to do?" Dorothea Forsyth asked plaintively.

"Well, some of you shove on your gardening gloves and cart away the shoots I chop off. Then there's the grass." She considered the narrow border that ran all round the bed. "You'd better see if Evvy will let us have some pairs of shears and tidy it up. You go and ask her, Barbara—and Kate. She's in the rock garden with some of the Fifth, I b'lieve."

"Will she *let* us have them, d'you think?" Barbara asked doubtfully. "Didn't she say we weren't unless she was there?"

"Tell her Burnie's coming and then she will," the resourceful Mary-Lou responded. "After all, they aren't like the secs, you know. You can hack yourself quite easily with *them*, but shears aren't nearly so dangerous."

"What will Burnie say about your scissors?" Ruth Barnes suddenly demanded of their leader, taking a rest from a struggle with an obstinate dandelion root.

"I don't know; but they aren't *secateurs*, anyway, and if the roses are left much longer, there won't *be* any next year—they'll all have gone to briar," Mary-Lou replied, not ceasing to wrestle with a tough shoot.

Ruth returned to her dandelion and conscientiously went on, delving for the end of the root. "I wish dandies wouldn't go down so *far!*" she lamented as she dug. "I must have gone down yards and I still haven't got to the end of the beastly thing!"

"They *are* beastly, aren't they?" Vi remarked sympathetically. "Look here! You come and have a go at this groundsel and I'll take over your dandy for a bit."

Ruth thankfully gave up the struggle and Vi squatted down on her heels and began to shovel out the earth round the recalcitrant root with a special trowel that was long and narrow.

It was a real gardening day, with a bright sun and a fresh breeze blowing off the sea. After their long imprisonment by the rain, they enjoyed themselves thoroughly, and when Miss Burnett, having got her netball teams well under way, arrived to see what they were doing, they were all hard at it.

"You're doing well," she said as she surveyed the piles of weeds that Emerence and the others were raking together in neat heaps while more forked them up into the barrows handled by Verity-Anne and her team. "Mind you don't trample down those chrysanthemums, Peggy. You're dangerously near them. Did Miss Everett say you might have those shears, by the way?"

Peggy Harper came to attention at this pointed question, a hurt look on her face. "Oh yes, Miss Burnett. We told her you would be coming and she said we might have them so long as we didn't fool with them."

Miss Burnett smothered a grin. "I see. Well, the grass certainly stands in much need of cutting. Don't mix it with those weeds, Verity-Anne. Don't you know better than that? Weeds go to the bonfire. Take the grass to Griffiths' grass heap at the back of the potting sheds. He'll want it for mulching later on."

Vi suddenly stood up, holding a long snakey looking white thing aloft with much triumph. "Miss Burnett! Look! Isn't he a whacker?"

"Good gracious, Vi! What a monster! That would take some getting-out!"

"Oh, well, Ruth did more than half of it," Vi explained honestly. "I only took over at the end. Can we keep it to show Miss Everett? I never saw such a huge dandy root in my life."

"Yes, if you like. Remember where you put it and be careful not to break it, though. I can't think how you managed to disinter it whole as it is." She then turned to other things. "Mary-Lou, what *are* you doing to those roses?"

"I'm cutting them down, Miss Burnett," Mary-Lou replied at her very meekest.

"But, my good child, *this* isn't the proper time of year to prune roses—or not bush roses. You ought to have left them till the end of February or early March. And I thought you children weren't supposed to touch the secateurs?"

76

"They're not secateurs; they're scissors."

"*What?* You come here at once and let me see what you've got hold of!" the mistress commanded.

Rather apprehensively, Mary-Lou swung round to come, only to find that she was caught by a long, strangling spray. Now every one of the girls knew perfectly well that when you were hooked by thorns your most sensible plan was to stand still and free yourself carefully and quietly. Mary-Lou knew it as well as anyone, but she lost her head. She began wrenching and twisting and promptly ripped the sleeve of her blouse from shoulder to elbow.

Miss Burnett simply ploughed over the bed to the rescue, shouting, "Stand still, you little featherhead! I'll free you in a moment."

She was almost on top of some Madonna lilies and, to avoid them, she took a leap over them and—vanished into the earth with a startled yell that was echoed by everyone present!

The horrified Middles rushed to the spot to peer down into a deep hole that for all they knew might go down to the centre of the earth. At any rate, they couldn't see the bottom. Neither could they see anything of Miss Burnett.

"It—it must have been an—an earthquake!" quavered Emerence.

"Don't talk nonsense, whoever that is!" came in sepulchral tones from the ground, causing them all to take a backward leap with wild shrieks. "It's some sort of old pit or well that has been filled in and the heavy rain has loosened the earth and my jumping on it has caused the whole thing to subside. That's all it is. Now one of you go and find Miss Everett and ask her to come here. And the rest of you don't dare to come within a yard of the place. You're sending mud and weeds right down on top of me."

They moved back and Verity-Anne, farthest away from the hole, went scudding off to the rock garden where she found Miss Everett.

"Please, Miss Everett, come at once!" she panted. "Miss Burnett has fallen into the pit!"

"*What?*"

"The pit—Miss Burnett's fallen into it and she sent me for you!"

"What pit?"

"The one in our garden bed—just beside the roses. Mary-Lou got caught in the thorns and Miss Burnett ran to help her, and she jumped and then she—she just vanished and she says it's a pit and we were to fetch you." Verity-Anne put things into a nutshell.

Miss Everett glanced round her own helpers who were standing listening open-mouthed to this story. "Katherine, Blossom and Hilary, run to the glass-houses and bring Griffiths. You can tell him what has happened. Lala Winterton, you go to the gym and bring me some of the ropes. You go with her, Meg. Elinor, Hilda and Amy, you go and find Jenks—I think he's at work in the orchard— and ask him to bring the longest apple-ladder. Move, all of you!—Oh, Betsy Lucy, you run and find Matron. Take Verity-Anne with you to tell her what has happened. Miss Burnett may have hurt herself, so Matron had better be prepared. Some of you Rangers had better go and bring one of your First Aid stretchers in case she's sprained an ankle and can't walk. The rest come with me."

Miss Everett tore over the ground at top speed. She arrived at the great square bed to find the younger girls huddled at a little distance from its centre and all looking scared out of their wits.

"Come off that bed at once and all of you keep on the path!" she ordered.

The frightened Middles did as they were told while she herself, picking her way cautiously, reached the great hole she could see in front of the rose bushes. Arrived there, she knelt down.

"Are you all right, Burnett?" she demanded, forgetting her audience in the exigency of the moment.

Greatly to her relief, Peggy Burnett replied, "Well, I'm not exactly comfortable. I rather think I've ricked an ankle and it's damp and chilly down here, but I'm neither killed nor seriously injured as your voice seems to imply. I shan't be sorry to get out, though. There's a tiny oozing of water coming from just below me, so I gather I've fallen into an old well that's been filled up some time, and the spring, or whatever it is, is beginning to function again."

"I've sent for ropes, ladders, Griffiths and Jenks, so we'll soon have you out of that."

"I'm glad to hear it." Peggy Burnett's voice was still cheerful but rather faint, and Miss Everett guessed that her ankle was hurting her pretty badly.

"I've sent to Matron, too, so she'll be ready to fix your ankle as soon as we can get you out—and that won't be long now," she added. "Here come the men and the apple-ladder."

Griffiths was the head gardener from Plas Howell, the real home of the school, so he was unable to say anything about the hitherto unsuspected well. He roped the ladder and then, with the help of Jenks, carefully lowered it. Once it was in position, Miss Everett went down it to find Miss Burnett, looking very white in the dim twilight of the well, leaning up against the wall with one foot doubled under her. There was a small puddle beneath her and when Miss Everett set her hand against the wall, she could feel drops slowly forming and oozing down.

"Well, we must get you out of this," she said briskly. "Let me see what I can do about that ankle. It's somewhat difficult, considering the restricted space, but I'll strap it up with my hanky. Then Griffiths and Jenks can come down and carry you up. Now don't begin fainting about here, please. There just isn't time or room for it. You'll get rheumatics if you stay much longer in this damp hole and I suppose you don't want that."

But she was growing rather more anxious about the flow of water which, even in the short space of time she had been there, seemed to her to be quickening.

"As if I'd be such a goop as to faint!" Miss Burnett retorted indignantly. "I must say, Everett, you're a complete mutt if—Ow!" For Miss Everett had taken advantage of her annoyance to draw the twisted foot from under her and the pain had been excruciating for the moment.

Miss Everett with a brief, "Set your teeth! This will hurt all right!" went to work as fast as she could.

Hurt it did, but Peggy Burnett set her teeth and when

it was over, though she felt slightly sick with the pain, her foot was really more comfortable. Miss Everett hurried up the ladder and spoke a few words to Griffiths.

He nodded when he heard of the water. "I'll go down, Miss. Jenks and you can steady the ladder. It'll be safer with one and she's small-like and I can handle her. I'm a fireman voluntary aid in me off time," he added with pride. "I knows the drill."

Down he went and picked up Miss Burnett as if she weighed no more than Verity-Anne. He slung her across his shoulders in fireman's lift; struck a match to verify the flowing of the water and then set off up the ladder, carefully, but as quickly as he could. Miss Everett had been quite right and, to his practised eye, it was plain that a very short time would see the spring gushing into its old outlet again.

When he reached the top, Miss Everett and Jenks were ready to take the semi-conscious Miss Burnett from him. They laid her down on the stretcher where Matron, who had joined the party, knelt down and administered a stiff dose of brandy. Griffiths had stayed to haul up the ladder. Then, muttering something about, "Get planks to lay across the mouth," he summoned Jenks and the pair went off with the ladder.

Matron ordered the Rangers to pick up the stretcher and bring it to San.

Four B were very subdued by what had happened, and when Griffiths came back with his planks the bed was naturally deserted. He produced a length of string to which was tied a metal footrule and lowered it carefully into the well. When he drew it up, he permitted himself a whistle, for the water had evidently cleared its vent by this time and already there was four inches. Then he laid his planks and set up a stake bearing a board on which he had chalked "DANGER."

As he went off again to his own quarters, he shook his head solemnly. "Forty feet if 'tis an inch!" he muttered to himself. "Them girls 'ull have to do their play-gardenin' somewheres else or mebbe we'll be 'avin' a drowndin' here!"

CHAPTER X

THE WELL

THE news of Miss Burnett's fall into the well spread like wildfire around the school, and set up a continual hum of young voices, each describing her part in the accident and subsequent rescue operation. Before anyone could say anything more, the gong sounded for Abendessen, so they had to stop talking and form into line to march to the dining-room. There, they were intrigued to see that Cherry Christy's stepfather, who was the owner of the island and also of Big House, was at the Staff table.

Cherry sat next to Doris Hill and Mary-Lou was opposite.

"What's your father doing here?" the latter craned across the table to ask as soon as they had sat down and the plates of fish and egg-sauce were beginning to circulate.

"Mary-Lou! Sit up and don't whisper across the table like that!" Bride Bettany who was at the head, serving, reproved her.

Mary-Lou sat back. "I only wondered why Mr. Christy was here," she said mildly. "You must agree, Bride, that it's rather unusual."

"Unusual or not, you aren't to behave like that at table," Bride told her firmly, choking back a laugh. Somehow, what would have been bare-faced cheek from most girls seemed quite natural in Mary-Lou. The others sometimes said resentfully that she got away with things that would have brought everyone down on *them* like a ton of bricks.

Cherry had no idea why her stepfather was there. She hadn't known that he was expected. She could guess, though. The whole school was buzzing with talk about the well and Miss Burnett's dramatic disappearance down it.

"I expect the Abbess sent for him to ask him about the well," she said. "—Oh, please, Bride, need I have such a big helping?"

The table settled down to enjoy its meal and Bride herself guided the chatter to the subject of Saturday's match. She had an idea that it might be as well not to leave the Middles to air their views about the afternoon's adventure when the owner of Big House was present.

In the meantime, the Staff table was also avoiding the subject. Mr. Christy's eldest girl, Dickie, who had been second prefect the previous year, was now at the new branch in the Oberland. Dickie Christy had been a favourite with everyone and he had brought her latest letter, full of news, for their delighting, so there was plenty to discuss and it was not until they were all seated in the school drawing-room, having their coffee, that he broached the question at all.

"I've brought the old maps," he said, laying them down on the small table by the Head. "I haven't had time to look at them and I don't remember any well shown there. Still, I haven't bothered much with them. However, we'll take a good look at them this evening."

"I hope we don't find any more filled-in wells," the Head said. "I shudder when I think of the way those children worked all over that bed throughout the summer! It was bad enough that poor Peggy Burnett should have fallen in. It would have been hair-raising if it had been one of the girls!"

"Most unlikely," he said soothingly. "In any case, I doubt if it would have occurred if we hadn't had all that rain. That's what did it, of course. By the way, I met your man on my way up and he tells me that he sounded it before he laid the planks over the mouth and there was four inches of water there already. I want to examine it properly tomorrow, but I rather think we shall find that it's filling rapidly. We must talk it over and decide what to do about it."

"Do about it!" the Head echoed. "I hope it'll be filled in again. Griffiths says it's forty feet deep if it's an inch!"

He laughed. "If we do decide to leave it open, I'll have a pump set up over it. It might be a good idea to have it in case we ever have another hot summer. You could always fall back on it for watering the garden. But whatever we finally do, you may be sure I shall see it is absolutely safe."

"Well, if you do that," the Head said doubtfully. "One may make rules, you know, but no one can guarantee that they'll be kept *all* the time."

"Meaning demons like that young What's-her-name you've had wished on to you?" he asked with a twinkle.

"I wasn't exactly thinking of Emerence. Small girls may forget all about rules in the excitement of a game and then—well, we don't want any tragedies, thank you."

"I'll see to that. If the thing's left, we'll make it all safe, I promise you. Now, wouldn't you like to see the maps?"

The maps were spread out and the excited Staff clustered round to examine them.

There were three, the first being comparatively modern, having been done at the beginning of the century. There was no sign of the well on it; nor did it appear in the second which had been drawn in the forties of the last century, when the orchard had been planted, but the well in the stableyard was marked.

"This must mean that it was filled in more than a hundred years ago," Miss Derwent, the new English mistress, commented. "I don't wonder it's subsided after all the rain we've had. What is the date of this third map, Mr. Christy?"

"1776," he replied. "My great-great-oh—five or six greats-grandfather had it done when he inherited. His mother was a great heiress, Delicia Lloyd, from whom, by the way, Dickie gets her name. It was she who brought St. Briavel's and the Carnbach estate into the family, together with a large fortune, most of which has gone down the drain by this time. We've always hung on to the island and what we could of Carnbach, though. Now, let's see."

He unrolled the parchment, stained and yellow with age, while the ink had turned brown. The Staff bent eagerly over it.

"There are a good many more trees here than now," Miss Annersley commented.

"Yes; my great-grandfather had most of those growing near the house cut down as he thought they made it damp."

"It's rather a miracle they could survive," Miss Stephens the geography mistress remarked.

"The house and park are in a dip, you remember. They were sheltered from the worst of the gales. At one time there was an artificial mound built across here—see. It's marked on this map." He pointed out a small shaded area.

"Why was that?" Rosalie Dene demanded.

"Well, not to protect the trees, you may be very sure. The family traditions say that it was built in the late seventeenth century by one of the Lloyds, who was more than suspected of being a freebooter, to hide his loot. If so, all I can say was he must have removed it later on, for no one has ever found anything worth mentioning, though the great Delicia's grandson had the mound dug away searching for it."

"Why?" asked two or three voices at once.

"He was the lad who lost most of the money. He was sent to Eton and Oxford, and whatever else he may have learned there, he learned to gamble. He couldn't dispose of the estate because it was very strictly entailed; but he sold everything else he could lay his hands on. He seems to have been consistently unlucky, for he died up to his neck in debt—he had other expensive tastes as well, I should explain—but luckily for all concerned, his only son, born after five girls, was only three or four when his father conked out, so he had a long minority as well as a pair of the most rigid trustees as ever took the job on."

"How do you mean—rigid?" Rosalie asked, looking up from the map which she had been studying with the greatest interest.

"They were a couple of grim old parsons and they flatly refused to pay any gambling debts, regardless of the code of polite society. They said they had enough to do to settle the legal accounts. However, thanks to their acumen and paring all expenses to the bone for some years, by the time the boy came of age, the estate was clear again and there was a small balance in the bank into the bargain."

"I hope he didn't repay them by gambling it away on the spot?" Miss Derwent said with interest.

"Not he! Between his trustees who were also his

guardians and his mother, and elder sisters who knew why life had to be so tight and resented it accordingly, young Michael was bred up to a horror of gambling that lasted to the day of his death. Moreover he never went to school, but had tutors, and when he came of age they married him off to a young lady with ten thousand of her own and as strict an upbringing as he had had. The pair spent their lives here, more or less, and though their three sons were allowed rather more freedom, they, too, kept clear of London and high society."

"That's understandable," Miss Annersley said. "I imagine the grandsons of the man whose executors had refused to pay his gaming debts would hardly be welcome there."

"Exactly! I've heard that more than one man came perilously near ruin as a result of that—Hello!" Rosalie Dene suddenly exclaimed. "Found it?"

"Yes, I think so. This is it, isn't it?" She laid her finger on a small circle.

He examined it closely. "Yes; that'll be it. Well, there we are, then. It must have been filled up some time between 1776 and 1843. I can look at the estate books and find out exactly when."

Rosalie was at the map again. "Look, Mr. Christy. What's this queer wavy line running from it?"

"No idea. Perhaps a path leading to some bygone shed or outhouse."

"It seems to finish at *this* place," Rosalie said, tracing the line with her finger. "See! Why, that'll be the hollow, won't it?"

Miss Everett took a hand. "Let's see, Dene. Yes; you're right. Probably they had sheds there. There seem to have been trees about it in those days. I suppose they were cut down at the same time as the others. There are only bushes now."

It was the best guess they could make, and as it was getting late, Commander Christy rolled up his maps, promised to see what details he could find from the records of the estate, though he warned them that it could not be done for a week or two as he was already very busy, and now must contact the water engineer over at Carnbach about the well and find out what he thought they should do about it.

"Very well," Miss Annersley agreed. "In the meantime, Griffiths can fence it off with barbed wire and the whole bed is to be out of bounds to everyone. Rosalie, don't forget to put up a notice to that effect before you go to bed. I will *not* run the risk of any more accidents. This term is being far too eventful for my taste!"

CHAPTER XI

THE PREFECTS HAVE AN ADVENTURE

THE Staff and Middles having been responsible for the latest sensation in the school, it was more than time for the Seniors to do their share. Furthermore, as it turned out, it was the prefects who proceeded to add to the list of surprises of that term.

After the heavy rains which had caused the subsidence in the well, the weather seemed to have made up its mind to reform. Day after day dawned with bright sunshine and blue skies flecked with little white curls of cloud that drifted gently across or else hovered peacefully in the heavens, for there was very little wind just then. In fact, as Loveday remarked one afternoon, it was really much more like late spring than the end of October and nearly half-term in the Christmas term.

Griffiths was loud in thankfulness for the well so startlingly discovered. Thanks to the lack of rain, there seemed to be risk of water shortage and the mainland authorities issued a warning about the need for conserving water supplies. With a forty-foot well at his disposal, the head gardener was able to do all the watering that was needful, even on a big place like this.

There was one drawback to the well. The spring seemed never-failing, but at no time did the water rise beyond ten feet from the top of the well. Griffiths thought that there must be an outlet which carried the water off, but where it went, no one could say. It made drawing it difficult, however, and Griffiths was looking forward to the pump which Commander Christy had decided must be erected.

The well itself had proved much deeper than he had reckoned by his own rough and ready methods; and the water engineer, when he had inspected it, said that there must have been a good deal of rubble at the bottom which the water was gradually scouring out, and he expected that in another year's time it would be found to be sixty feet deep with some fifty feet or so of water. Griffiths was jubilant about it, but Miss Annersley was far from pleased. She had visions of her lambs falling in and being drowned. Pending the erection of the pump, she had the whole bed heavily fenced round with barbed wire, and all sorts of horrid penalties were promised to anyone who was caught inside the fence.

Commander Christy was still much too busy to hunt through the old record for information, though he promised to see to it at the first opportunity. Meanwhile, he suggested that the Staff might like to have the old map to study at their leisure. He sent it up one morning together with the news that a small brother had arrived for the Christy girls—Dickie, Cherry and little Gay, who was five and at St. Agnes' with the rest of the Juniors.

The news of the Christy baby quite ousted the excitement about the well and Cherry was very indignant because she was not allowed to go home on the spot to see her mother and the new baby.

"You're better off than Dickie," Miss Annersley told her. "She must wait until Christmas, but you are going to see him on Saturday. Run along and you can have the fun of telling the news to the others and that must do for you until Saturday."

When Cherry came back on the Sunday night, having been given leave for the weekend, she was wildly excited.

"What's he like?" demanded Mary-Lou who, thanks to living next door to the Maynards where babies swarmed, considered herself a connoisseur of babies.

"He's *sweet!* Very tiny and his eyes are as blue as

Mummy's. He has lovely fair curls, too, all over his head. He's to be called Francis Michael 'cos Mummy's first name is Frances. Uncle Kester is to be his godfather and Dickie will be his godmother. Uncle Kester is flying her home next weekend for the christening. Isn't she *lucky?*"

"Ooh! I should just think she *is!*" breathed Doris enviously.

"Pooh! That's nothing!" This was Emerence with her nose in the air. *"I* flew all the way from Australia."

Mary-Lou eyed her limpidly. "I don't think I'd care about all that amount of flying," she said. "You miss such a lot."

The bell rang for prayers just then, so they had to stop talking.

It was the next Monday that the prefects contributed their little effort. When they finished lessons at four o'clock, they asked leave of the Head to take a stroll about the grounds after tea. She gave leave at once, for it was not their games' day and as Miss Burnett was still *hors de combat*, they had had no gym.

Accordingly, having had their tea, they assembled in the court-yard at the back of the house, clad in shoes and long coats, for though the days were still unseasonably warm, the evenings were beginning to be chilly.

"Which way shall we go?" Loveday asked.

"Through the orchard and round to the playing-field. Then cut across past the Hollow and come right round and through the rock garden," Bride suggested. "That would give us a decent stretch and we've just time to do it comfortably."

No one else had anything better to suggest, so they set off, Loveday leading with Anne Webster. The rest followed in two bunches, one led by Tom Gay and Julie Lucy and the other, consisting of Bride, Nancy and Primrose, coming a little way behind them. They were talking of their missing fourth, for these three and Elfie had come to the school together and worked side by side the whole way through.

Bride was still disposed to be mournful at her loss. This evening, however, she was soon gossiping about the well, the Christy baby and a letter she had had from Canada from her beloved Aunt Jo.

The way to the orchard led through the shrubbery at the end of which came the five-barred gate to the orchard. Most of the apples had been picked by this time, but they found a few windfalls which they salvaged and went on, munching enjoyably. A gate at the far end took them into what was known as the paddock where a cow and two or three sheep kept the grass down. From this they climbed a stile and were at the far end of the playing-field.

This was almost the highest part of the estate and they had been going uphill all the way. From here, they could turn and see, beyond the treetops of the orchard, a glimpse of the sea with the glorious colours of an October sunset reeling across the sky.

While Loveday and Anne paused to enjoy this, the five games experts went off to examine the hockey-pitch which was suffering from the lack of rain.

Audrey Simpson, the hockey captain, inspected it anxiously. "You know," she said, "if we don't have rain soon, this simply won't be fit to play on. We shan't run— it'll mean sliding, and that'll be nice with the Sacred Heart team coming over on Saturday!"

"Couldn't Griffiths do something about watering it?" Lesley Pitt suggested. "He's got all the water he needs in that blessed well. Surely he could manage something?"

"How d'you propose to set about it?" Audrey demanded. "It's a lot bigger than any flowerbed, and it's too far from the well for him to rig up the sprinkler as he's done for the front lawn."

"What about the stirrup-pumps?" Nancy suggested. "Couldn't we all hoe in with them and buckets and spray it that way? The laxe pitch will have to be seen to as well, for it's quite as bad. Thank Heaven our Saturday match is an Away one and the state of *that* pitch will have to be someone else's headache! But the Lucy Guest Foundation team comes the Saturday after. Let's hope it rains between then and now!"

"How shall you manage about half-term?" Julie queried.

"Same as the hockey team are managing. Both matches are in the morning and we'll go off as soon as they're over. It's a nuisance, of course, but it couldn't be helped. There just wasn't another Saturday free and the Sacred Heart have their half-term this weekend and the Carnbach Grammar the weekend after."

Loveday suddenly woke up to her responsibilities at this point and glanced at her watch. She gave an exclamation. "We ought to be going back. The sun's gone and it's growing dark quickly now. If you want to go round by the Hollow and the rock garden, we'd better make a start. That rock garden is a regular mantrap in the dark these days!"

"It's those wretched kids, Madge and Hilary in Lower VB, we have to thank for that," Julie said disgustedly. "They went mad over the rock garden last term and what they've done to what was a simple oblong with a rockery all round it, flagged paths and a few beds here and there, is just no one's business! They've got little bits of rockery dotted all over the place, and standard roses and clumps of tall flowers with stakes to match! And as if that wasn't enough, they had to go and get leave to make a fish pond at the far end! Those kids have no idea of moderation!"

"Oh, well, we can avoid their precious fish pond," Loveday said soothingly. "We can go up the centre steps and come out by the front path and go round that way. Then we shan't go near the fish pond. But I do think we ought to be moving now."

The girls realised that she was right. The last of the sunset colours had faded from the sky and the sea looked cold and grey and was darkening fast under the darkening clouds. The grandees of the school turned away from the pitches and began to stroll onwards down the field to the little path that led downhill to what was always known as The Hollow.

This was a dip in the ground, roughly oval in shape, with bushes of garden azaleas and fuchsias growing about it. Miss Everett always declared that some time or other it must have been dug out for a special purpose as its shape was far too regular to be natural. The younger girls frequently picnicked there in the summer when such things were allowed. At one end, the ground sloped up to a little hillock, down the short, slippery turf of which the Juniors loved to slide with small regard for the resulting mess to their clothes. At the other, there was a kind of sunk grassy path with the remains of what the school took to have been a summer house at its entrance to the Hollow. The path, as was shown in the 1776 map of the estate, led from the part of the garden where the form flowerbeds were. The prefects would not use the path, for their way lay nearer the house and to go round by it would mean that they would certainly be much later than six in going in. They would cross it, go across the rough pasturage that lay here and then reach the shrubbery.

When they reached the head of the downhill path, some evil genius suggested a race to Bride. She was beginning to feel a little chilly, for a wind was rising which blew off the sea and was cold.

"Let's race to the shrubbery," she said. "The kids can't see us and we haven't had much exercise today."

The others fell in with the idea at once. They lined up as well as they could, with Julie and Nancy, the shortest of them, in front. Loveday gave the word, reminding them that they had better not try to jump the sunk path as it was growing dark. Then she gave the word and off they went, racing at top speed down the slope, across the rough grass and then scrambling down the bank to the sunk path.

Julie, who despite her lack of inches, was swift on her feet, was well ahead, with long-legged Tom Gay behind; then Bride and Primrose and the rest streaming after. Julie took a wild leap into the centre of the path from the bottom of the bank and Tom took a wilder one and landed on all fours at its farther side. Bride and Primrose were not far behind and the four yells that followed their landing might almost have been heard at Big House.

The people who had just reached the top of the bank managed to check themselves, but the rest were carried on and the result was that six prefects found themselves wallowing in a sticky, clinging mud that had certainly not been there the day before when they had sauntered along in that direction.

"Mud," shrieked Bride, who had grabbed hold of a hazel growing near by and was trying to drag her feet out of the mess. "How's it gone muddy at this time of year?"

No one bothered to answer, for her fellow-sufferers were much too busy trying to struggle out and the girls on the bank were scrambling down to hold out helping hands to them.

Bride contrived to yank her feet clear, but she finally landed at the top of the bank again with about a couple of pounds of smelly clay sticking to each shoe and had to sit down, pull them off and scrape away what she could with a twig.

Tom, who had fallen half-way up the opposite bank, was able to free herself fairly easily, though her shoes and stockings were a sight to behold. Primrose was hauled out by main force, exerted by Loveday and Nancy; but Julie, caught in the very centre, was another story.

"It's *wet!*" she gasped as she fought to free herself from the clinging mud. "Ow! I can't get out! Give me a hand, someone!"

"D-don't go t-too far d-down!" Primrose warned with chattering teeth, for between the shock of finding mud there at all together with feet and ankles soaked and muddy, she was shivering. Besides, now that the sun had gone in, the wind felt cold.

Loveday went as far as she could to the bottom of the bank, extended one hand, clutching a stout hazel-branch with the other and just managed to catch Julie's fingers in sailor's grip. She pulled valiantly and Julie struggled and twisted, but all to no purpose.

"I—I'm going in deeper!" she said suddenly in very shaky tones.

Loveday glanced round. Bride had pulled off her shoes and stockings and was scrubbing her feet with her handkerchief.

"Bride! Come and give a hand!" the Head Girl said sharply.

Big, sturdy Bride exclaimed at her tone; but she jumped up and padded cautiously down to where Loveday was clinging to the bush.

"What's up? Julie stuck? O.K. Can you change to her other hand. Then I'll grab the hazel at the other side and catch this. Don't look so scared, Julie. We'll have you out of that in half a sec, now. That's right; let go of Loveday and hang on to me."

Bride was half a head taller than Loveday and her arms were much longer. She was able to grip poor, frightened Julie much more firmly and give her confidence. Meanwhile, Tom Gay had rushed off to the playing-field again, clearing the sunk path with a bound that would not have disgraced a kangaroo. She remembered that one of the tug-o'-war ropes had been left in the little shed where they kept the marker and a few other oddments. It was unlocked, so she had no trouble in collecting her rope and was back just as the rest were beginning to feel worried, for all the hauling and goodwill of Loveday and Bride could not drag Julie one inch to the bank: she was more than ankle-deep in the mud now and her own struggles were causing her to sink every moment.

"Julie! Stop that squirming!" Tom ordered as Primrose and Audrey set off to go round the bed as hard as they could and get someone in authority to come to their aid. "Stand up as straight as you can and keep still."

While she talked, her fingers were busy, making a running noose in the rope. Now it was done and she stood up. "I'm going to throw this over you. Pull it tight round your waist and we'll haul you out that way. Now; are you ready?—Move a bit to the side, Loveday. You can let go her hand, Bride's got the other safe. Coming *up!*"

The rope flew out and the noose descended fair and square over Julie's head. With the free hand, she dragged it down to her waist and Tom gave a sharp pull and it tightened.

"Now!" Tom straddled to get a firm stance. "You stay where you are, Bride, and hang on to her. Loveday—and you, Nancy and Lesley and Anne, join on behind me. Anne, you're the heaviest. You take the end. Are you ready? *Pu-u-ull!*"

They hauled with every ounce of their strength. Julie shrieked for she felt as if the rope was cutting her in two.

93

Bride gripped her hand firmly and yanked as hard as she could. For one awful second even this seemed to have no effect. Then there came a melancholy "Gloo-op!" Her feet left the mud so suddenly that she sprawled helplessly forward on her face and they were able to draw her to the bank, where she scrambled to her feet with a helping hand from Bride who had stood by her stoutly.

She was white-faced and shivering violently. Her coat and skirt were inches thick in the glutinous mud and her shoes had been left behind; but apart from this and the shock, she was all right.

"We must get her back as quickly as possible and Matey will see to her," Loveday said, rallying her forces as quickly as she could.

"I'm all right!" Julie said as steadily as she could for chattering teeth. "Anyhow, I don't want Matey fussing round!"

"It isn't what you want; it's what you get, my child," Lesley informed her. "Audrey and Prim went haring off to find the Head, so Matey will know all about it, never you fear! Can you walk? If so, come on! Bride, you take that side and I'll have this. Heavens! How that mud does stink! Come on! She shouldn't stand about!"

Bride and Lesley gripped the reluctant Julie firmly on either side and marched her off at a pace she declared she couldn't keep up.

"Oh yes, you can," Bride retorted bracingly. "Keep her going, Lesley. It'll warm her and there'll be less risk of a chill."

"I wish—you—wouldn't t-talk—as if I w-was deaf and n-not all there!" Julie panted as they hurried her along.

"You save your breath and stop talking!" was all the satisfaction she got.

They had reached the beds and were turning along the path that led to the shrubbery when Audrey and Primrose came racing back, followed by Miss Annersley and Matron. The wind was blowing harder and the "angel's wings" of Matron's cap streamed wildly behind her. As they reached the trio struggling along, the Head gave a cry.

"Who is that?" She switched on the powerful torch she

was carrying, for it was nearly dark now and they could see the windows of Big House all twinkling with lights. *"Girls!"* as her eyes fell on the mud-caked Julie. "Never mind now! Quick to the house with her! Are the rest of you all right?"

"All O.K., ta!" In the excitement of it all, Tom had lost her head and spoke to the Head as she would never have dreamed of doing in her normal senses. "Even Julie's only had a fright and lost her shoes and muddied her clothes."

Miss Annersley shared in the excitement. She never noticed Tom's lapse. She pushed Bride to one side and took her place. "Off you go and into a hot bath with you at once! Come along, Lesley! We must get Julie back at once. Anyone else who fell in, hurry on and have a hot bath, too. I'll see you all later."

They obeyed at once and by the time Julie had been more or less rushed up to San., all the others who had sampled the mud were in hot baths while the rest were hurriedly changing.

By seven o'clock, Julie was safely between hot blankets, while the others were dressed and had been summoned in a body to the study to tell their tale to the accompaniment of milky coffee.

When she had heard all they could tell her, Miss Annersley sat back for a moment or two, considering. Nothing could be done that night. It was pitch dark and even with torches they could hardly hope to see much. She finally told the girls that all prep would be excused. They might go to the library and read until Abendessen.

They were not ungrateful. As Loveday said next day, they felt all-in and they certainly couldn't have done any work worth calling work after the shock they had had. The Head knew that of course. She had marked the white faces of Bride and Nancy and Primrose and the heavy eyes of all and realised that preparation would be useless with them. As it was, thanks to her common sense, they managed to recover a little before they went to bed and once they were there, Matron arrived with her favourite nostrum, hot milk, and saw that they drank it, with the result that not even Bride and Loveday suffered from nightmare as they confidently expected, and apart from a slight, interesting pallor, even Julie was more or less herself next day.

CHAPTER XII

UNLOOKED-FOR DISCOVERY

"WHAT do you think it is, Griffiths?" Miss Annersley was standing on the bank above the sunk path, Griffiths at her side, examining the scene of last night's adventure.

Griffiths stared solemnly down. The "path" was an inch deep in water now; the grass and daisies still showing bravely were being slowly drowned; and if you listened intently, you could hear a faint rippling sound which meant that more water was coming to join the other. Commander Christy, who had come in answer to an urgent 'phone call, also looked at the gardener. To his own mind, there was only one explanation and he was interested to see if the big Welshman would come to it on his own.

Griffiths turned, presently, and strode along to the Hollow. Treading cautiously, he scrambled down the sloping bank and, feeling with the toe of his boot at each step, he began to make towards the centre of the Hollow. At one point, about three yards from the side, there came a squishing sound as he gingerly set his foot down. The water was not visible yet, but it was coming—not a doubt of it. He backed carefully and climbed back up the bank to where his companions were waiting for him.

"Well, Miss," he said in his soft, Welsh voice, "this is where the overflow goes—aye, yes indeed. There was a brook, look you, and it ran into this hollow which was made big for a pond. Mebbe they had ornamental ducks on it. Now the well's cleared again and the spring's free, the water's seeping up as well as coming from the overflow and this'll be a pond again." With his ham of a hand, he indicated the Hollow. "Now look you, we must make another overflow at this end so as not to have stagnant water here. Mebbe there was one some time?" He looked a query at the Commander.

That gentleman shook his head. "There wasn't—or not as far back as the records go. That was the main reason why they had the well filled in."

The Head turned to him in surprise. "Do you really *know* that?"

He nodded. "After I had your call last night, I hunted out the early records. Matter-of-fact," he added with a grin, "I was up till four this morning, reading 'em. Mighty interesting!"

"They must have been!" Miss Annersley said drily.

"They certainly *were!* Among other things, I found that the well was filled in and the pond and brook drained by Delicia Lloyd three years after her marriage. They had no overflow and the water became stagnant. Naturally, they got mosquitoes and, in the autumn, unpleasant miasmas. She had twin girls within the first year of her marriage. When the twins were about two, there was a terribly hot summer and the poison breathing from the marsh this became, set up a kind of low fever which attacked one person after another. The twins went down and died within twelve hours of each other. Her husband took it and was only dragged through by the skin of his teeth. Finally, a young maid died."

"Oh, the poor soul!" Miss Annersley cried. "What a tragedy!"

"You may say so. There was another baby by that time —a boy. Delicia was terrified lest he should get it, too, so she sent for a local wise man who seems to have merited his title. He told her that they would never be free of the fever until the water was driven from the land, for the noxious vapours that rose from it brought the fever from the bowels of the earth."

"All quite true," the Head said thoughtfully, "though not exactly as *he* meant it. If we can't make an overflow, the well must be closed again. I daren't risk the girls!"

He took no notice of this for the moment, but went on

97

D

with his story. "The well was filled in and the brook and pond drained. They had cartloads of sand and earth brought and flung down and some loads of gravel as well. The brook and the pond basin were roughly filled up and her husband recovered. There was no more of that particular fever here again and she had no need to fear it for her son."

"The poor soul!" Miss Annersley said pitifully. "Well, to get back to the present day, I suppose that through the years what they put in to fill up the Hollow and the sunk path gradually settled, which accounts for their present shape today?"

"So far as I can gather, they seem to have done nothing but empty the stuff in and leave it. None of the succeeding generations have bothered their heads about it."

"I suppose that as long as the spring was choked, it was all right?" the Head said thoughtfully.

"As I see it, the freeing of the spring has set the whole thing going again. Nothing would happen, of course—at least, I don't think so—until the water had reached the level of the overflow. But as soon as that happened, it began seeping through, as Griffiths says. Probably if we hadn't had the last two or three weeks of dry weather, we should have seen it happening much sooner. As it is, it took your prefects with their gazelle feats to discover it."

"What are you going to do about it now?"

"I must have the experts over again. I can't tell you yet."

"I see. Meantime, we don't want any more frights like last night's."

"Certainly not. We'll have the whole thing wired off for the moment. I'll get on to Archer—the man I had before—and get him to come along for the weekend. If he thinks it can be done we'll have an overflow cut at the far end. The only trouble is that the land rises there, so it'll mean cutting down and using drain-pipes to the ditch in the lane leading to Kittiwake Cove."

"Won't that be a terribly expensive job?"

He looked thoughtful. "It may—and it may not. All depends on what we find when we start cutting." He

98

turned to Griffiths. "Get the place wired off, will you? I'll send old Pugh along to give you a hand with it. Miss Annersley, I should issue a 'No Trespass' against this part of the world until that's done. Once it is, it'll be safe enough." He paused and moved along to the remains of the so-called summer-house. "You know, I've often wondered why anyone wanted to build a summer-house just here. It's nowhere near the garden proper and there's not much of a view. Now, of course, I understand."

"Do you mean they had it built as a kind of boat-house?—Oh, but the Hollow, even at its fullest, wouldn't give anyone much fun with rowing. It's not nearly large enough."

"Not a house of any kind. This," he slapped the butt of a post round which hung the hoary beauty of Old Man's Beard, "is the remains of a rustic *bridge.*"

Griffiths gave vent to a hoarse chuckle. He had thought of that one himself. Miss Annersley gasped.

"A *bridge?*"

"Yes; in wet weather the ground hereabouts must often have been badly flooded, even though there was this hillock. This is the most direct route to the village, so no doubt the bridge was built to save having to go round by the main road every time. You can see how far it must have run into the bank." He measured the distance with his eye. "A good eight feet or so. Like you, we always thought that some romantic soul must have built an arbour here and this was one of the main posts. It's clear enough now, though, what it was. Of course, once the water had been drained off, there was no further need for a bridge so the structure was left to wind and weather and rotted away in time—all but this stump."

There was no more to be said. Commander Christy gave Griffiths a few more directions about the wiring and then he and Miss Annersley went up to the house where they parted, he to go home and send his own handyman across to help Griffiths, and she to request Rosalie Dene to put up notices that no one might go near the Hollow and the sunk path until further notice.

"But why not?" Hilary Wilson of Lower V B demanded

of a select company of her own special friends in the form.

No one knew, for no one had heard what had happened to the prefects the previous evening, the Head having asked them to keep the whole affair to themselves for the present. She had to be satisfied with the bare fact that the area was forbidden. Lower V B were a law-abiding crowd on the whole, so they only grumbled among themselves and then forgot the question in exchanging notes on what they hoped to do with their half-term.

Lower IV B were not nearly so easily satisfied. They groused loudly and thoroughly and one or more of the brighter spirits even suggested that they should go as near as they could and see what was going on, and if they happened to go rather nearer than they ought, well, that was just an accident!

Mary-Lou, as form prefect, promptly squashed this. "Just you let me catch you doing anything so rotten," she said, glaring at Emerence from whom the suggestion had come.

"Okay, then. If I want to go I'll just go, and hang the row!"

"Oh, no, you won't—not if you want to spend half-term with me instead of here. What do you think the Head is? You'd jolly well have *no* half-term; and serve you right, too!"

Emerence subsided at this. Most of the school happened to be going away for half-term and then Mary-Lou heard that Emerence was condemned to staying at school, together with Carola Johnstone. So she had begged leave to telephone her mother and Mrs. Trelawney had asked for the Head and given her an invitation for those two. Emerence was looking forward to it and she guessed by what Mary-Lou had said that if she broke rules, she would not be allowed to go, and such a thing was unthinkable.

She decided to behave herself and, when Friday morning came, went off with the rest in high feather. The only people left behind were the teams who must remain until after their matches, both of which took place at half-past nine next morning, so that they too would be off by mid-day. The Head, who believed in taking no risks, sent them all off to Carnbach for the day in charge of Rosalie Dene and Biddy O'Ryan, both of whom were also staying till next day. Rosalie had several oddments to see to and Biddy was refereeing for the lacrosse team. Miss Burnett, who was now able to get about, would referee for the hockey and then go to Cardiff, whence she was flying to Aberdeen to spend the week-end.

Rosalie took the school car, ran her Head and Miss Burnett to Cardiff where they parted, and Biddy, who had the use of the Maynards' runabout, set off in the opposite direction, for she was staying with an old school-friend.

Many times during the week-end, spent with her cousin Wing-Commander Edgar Mordaunt and his invalid wife, did Miss Annersley's thoughts stray to Big House and the surprising developments of the present term. She enjoyed herself in Gloucester, but it was with a very youthful thrill of excitement that she waved good-bye to Edgar Mordaunt as the train left Gloucester station. She was meeting Rosalie Dene at Cardiff and the pair would go home by car from there.

Miss Dene had brought her a letter which she handed over almost before the pair of them sat down in a café. She seemed mildly excited herself, and, as she glanced down the closely written sheet, Miss Annersley grew excited, too.

"Well, this *is* a surprise!" she exclaimed when she had finished reading. "You know what it says, don't you, Rosalie?"

Rosalie nodded. "Seeing I brought it myself—They live in Dad's new parish and I went along to see them yesterday. This was handed to me for you. I told them I knew it would be all right, so the prefects are in for a special thrill tomorrow." She laughed as she ended and Miss Annersley laughed too.

"A very pleasant thrill, for once," she said pensively when she had sobered down and the coffee had come. "After all that's happened during the past half-term, that's a shock in itself. Never in my life have I known such a crowded period!"

"Oh, I don't know that I'd say just that," Rosalie replied

thoughtfully. "Jo gave us some pretty crowded times in her day."

"Yes; but she spread them rather more. Well, perhaps this last half of the term will be a little quieter."

"We'll hope so. By the way, I've thought of something."

"Oh? What is it?" The Head eyed her with interest.

"Why, if we only have a decent frost, we shall be able to do a spot of skating this year. We'll have our own pond and the brook as well and I don't suppose either will be deep enough to be dangerous."

"Most unlikely. Michael Christy told me that he doubted if the pond would be more than four feet deep at the deepest part. But, my dear girl, have you forgotten that we live on an island?"

"What's that got to do with it? Rosalie demanded, surprised.

"Only that it's not very likely we shall have frost hard enough to make the ice fit for skating. It's the salt in the air, I fancy."

Rosalie laughed. "If we have a winter anything like the last we're bound to have *some* skating. Do you remember what happened when Biddy O'Ryan took the Fifth Forms to the cliff above Kittiwake Cove?"

The Head gurgled with laughter at that memory. "I have not—nor Matron's wrath when she saw what Tom and Annis had done to their stocking-knees. Oh, how she raged about it!"

"By the way," Rosalie said, changing the subject again, "have you heard how Mrs. Bettany is?"

"Better, for the time being; but I'm afraid it's going to mean an operation. I was on the 'phone to the Quadrant yesterday and got Peggy—Kester Bellever had flown her over with Dickie and she's to stay for the next ten days or so. She said her father was taking her mother to London to see Grafton Mann and they will abide by his decision. Poor Bride! It won't have been a very happy half-term for her! I was sorry for Elfie's disappointment. She had expected Bride for half-term, you may remember."

"Elfie will understand better than most. She was at the Templemore station for a word with Bride when they changed trains. I saw the pair of them going off together. The Wintertons had young Maeve with them, so Bride must have expected Elfie."

"Elfie has behaved very well. She's a fine girl and Bride is another. My dear, we'd better go. It gets dark soon now and I want to be at Big House before dark if it's possible. I want to see what they've decided."

At Big House itself they found Commander Christy waiting for them, his face full of suppressed excitement.

"What's happened next?" Miss Annersley demanded with an apprehensive movement of her hands, almost as if she were warding off a blow.

"Nothing's happened—nothing that need worry you," he replied quickly.

She drew a long breath. "Thank Heaven for that! How are Carey and the baby?"

"Both splendid. Carey's gaining every day and he's as sturdy as they make 'em."

"I'm so glad. Did the christening go off well?"

"Splendidly. Blinkie nearly yelled the place down, so the devil went out of him all right!"

"*What?*"

"Don't you know that old yarn? They always say that if a baby doesn't yell when the water's poured, the devil hasn't gone. It's supposed to be the devil yelling at the touch of Holy Water."

"What tripe!" This was Rosalie. "I should say the devil's a good deal too knowing to be caught that way anyhow."

"Well, the deed is done and my son is now a Christian. Don't you want to know what we found when we started cutting?"

"Of course we do; but we had to be polite and ask about Carey and the boy. What *have* you found? Your ancestor's ill-gotten gains, by any chance?" Miss Annersley asked lightly.

"Come along and see!"

"Very well. Never mind the car, Rosalie. You come and see, too."

They left the car standing before the house and went

through the shrubbery and across the rough pasture which was the quickest way to the place where the 'sunk path' began. It was there no longer, but a gay little streamlet babbled downhill where it had been. They walked along the bank to where it ran into the Hollow, and there was a rough bridge made of four planks with a handrail of rope flung across it.

"Only a temporary affair," the owner of the place said, nodding at it. "It'll do for the moment, seeing you haven't any babies here to fall through into the water. I suppose I'm right in saying that your younger girls won't be allowed here without someone in charge for the present? Yes; I thought so! There's our pond." He waved his hand towards the shallow pool that covered the bottom of the Hollow with one or two tiny islands where there had been bumps in the ground just showing above the water. "Archer found it had a layer of clay beneath, so nothing will seep through. That's why it isn't anything like at its proper level yet. Come on, see the latest."

He hurried them round the pond and finally halted them beside another tiny brook which rippled down the gentle slope towards a circular brick tunnel, which to Miss Annersley's certain knowledge she had never seen before. She exclaimed with surprise:

"Do you really mean you've managed to get all this done during the week-end? How on earth did you do it?"

"No fear! When Archer came, he declared that at some time or other there *must* have been another outlet. We set Griffiths and the rest to digging just here at the end of the hillock and came on this, six feet below the surface. We've got it cleared as far as the ditch, so the water can get away safely; but actually, it goes much farther on. You see it's four feet in diameter? Archer says that, judging by the brickwork and the remains of an iron sluice we found about three feet down it, it was done in the late fifteenth century. They'd just begun to use brick round about that time. We haven't got the farther end cleared, of course; there hasn't been time. But Archer feels fairly sure that we shall find it comes out somewhere along the Kittiwake Cove cliffs."

"Not really? How very thrilling!"

He gave her a disgusted look. "Oh, come, Hilda! Aren't you any brighter than that? Jo Maynard would have been on to it in a flash!"

"Jo has a lurid imagination which I have *not*!" Miss Annersley retorted. "No; beyond a good outlet for the water, which I don't think your ditch is, I don't in the least see what you're driving at."

"Why, who did all this filling up—incidentally causing the pond to turn stagnant, and indirectly bringing about the deaths of those babies and that poor young maid? Dai Lloyd, of course, the freebooter and pirate! I've said nothing yet to Archer, but it wouldn't surprise me in the least if we found that that old scoundrel had used the drain to hide his ill-gotten goods and had had it all filled in later. Don't you see? He could have the stuff brought round to the cove by boat and it would be easy enough to rig up some sort of lifting tackle. He had only to drain the pond and close the well's overflow for a day or two. Then he could crawl through the drain, fix up his tackle and haul the stuff up and bury it somewhere close to the mouth of the other outlet. After that, he had this end all filled in and the mound which, by the by, ended in the hillock, built up. He never married. When he died, the estate came to a great-great-nephew who had been brought up somewhere near the marches, Ludlow way, I think. This man had never seen the old man or the place and would know nothing about it till he got here. I expect Dai set his sailors on the job, for there has never been any hint that the villagers knew anything about it. We *do* know that his boat, the *Seahawk*, was hanging about St. Briavel's for two or three days and then sailed and was never heard of again, nor any of her crew, either, except the mate, who turned up about six weeks later. If, as I think, that happened *after* he had buried his booty, then there was every reason for the *Seahawk*'s vanishing like that in calm summer weather. 'Dead men tell no tales' may be a truism, but like most of 'em, it's a sane idea."

The women stared at him aghast as they saw the implications of his story.

"Do you mean," Rosalie almost whispered at last, "that you think he got the mate to sink her *on purpose*? But— that would be neither more nor less than cold-blooded mass-murder!"

"From all accounts, Dai Lloyd wouldn't think twice about a little detail of that kind. I told you he was a pirate. He almost certainly had at least a score of other murders on his conscience—if he had such a thing. At any rate, the mate turned up six weeks later, as I told you, and the pair of beauties lived together until the mate died, when Dai carried on alone for another two or three years. He was found dead—*very* dead—when no one had seen or heard anything of him for a few months and the vicar of the parish insisted on going to see if he were ill or hurt."

"Good gracious!" Miss Annersley stopped there.

"Well, they've all been gone over three hundred years now and no doubt are expiating their sins yet. But don't you see: this accounts for nothing turning up when that other precious forebear of mine had most of the mound dug away. He never found the treasure because it was never there. If Dai and his boon companion didn't squander it all in riotous living, then it is still lying snugly hidden somewhere along the cliffs of Kittiwake Cove and we still have to find it!"

CHAPTER XIII

UNEXPECTED VISITOR

HAVING administered his shock, and feeling quite satisfied with the results, Commander Christy said good-bye shortly after and tramped off home leaving Miss Annersley and Miss Dene to return somewhat dazedly to the Big House. Whatever else they had expected from the work of Mr. Archer, they had certainly not expected anything like this.

On the way, the Head turned to her secretary. "Not a word of all this to anyone, Rosalie! We should have half the Middles trying to squirm down that pipe in search of treasure!"

Rosalie was in complete agreement. "I only hope Commander Christy hasn't let Cherry know anything about it," she said.

"I'd forgotten Cherry. Merciful Heavens! What do we do now?" Something very like consternation was in the Head's voice. "If Cherry knows anything about this, it'll be all over the Middles and we shall have to appoint watchdogs, one for each of the worst demons!"

"I'd better ring them up when I've taken my things off and ask him," Rosalie said as they turned down the path to the shrubbery. "If he hasn't, I can beg him to say nothing. If he has——"

"If he *has*," Miss Annersley interrupted with emphasis, "You must impress it on him to forbid her to mention it to anyone."

"Very well. Anyhow," Rosalie added as they reached the shrubbery, "they will have the Christmas play to think of in a week or so, and that's a mercy! Isn't Lady Russell doing it herself this year?"

"So she said when she last wrote. I expect it next week— if this news about Mrs. Bettany hasn't upset things altogether."

"Not a thing like that, it won't. Lady Russell never has let the school down and I'm certain she never will. Have you any idea what form the play is to take?"

"None; so it's no use asking me. She didn't go into any details when she mentioned it. She simply said that as Jo had her hands full with two tiny babies, she was doing it herself this year and would send it as soon after halfterm as possible."

They had reached the end of the shrubbery and taken the turn to the gravelled walk under the front windows of the Big House. It was almost dark now, but lights here and there from the windows made it possible to see the path, though they had to pay attention to their feet until they had nearly reached the great door which stood open, letting the glow from the hall lamp stream across the steps. Then Rosalie stood stock still with a shriek of horror.

"The car's gone! Look! It just isn't there!"

"I expect Griffiths or someone has run it round to the garage," the Head said serenely. "Don't yell like that, either. You nearly made me jump out of my skin. Even if anyone had stolen it, he certainly wouldn't get far. Didn't you tell me when we were crossing on the ferry that the petrol was running very low?"

Rosalie began to laugh. "It was so low, that I wondered if we would manage to get here on what was left. I meant to have filled up at Carnbach, but there wasn't any time unless we missed the ferry, so I hoped for the best—and, luckily, we did contrive to arrive."

"Then I expect Griffiths has called one of the other men and pushed her round. Anyhow, you can go and see, if you like, while I ask Megan for tea. But I'm not worried myself. Car thieves don't flourish on the island."

This was true, but in any case, something happened at that moment that drove the car completely out of their minds. A slender graceful figure appeared on the step and peered anxiously up and down. The Head gave it one look and then cleared what was left of the path in about three steps.

"Madge Russell!" she cried as she caught the newcomer in her arms. "Madge Russell! It's not *you*?"

"Me myself, large as life and a hundred times as natural! Oh, Hilda, it *is* good to be back with you again, even for a short time!" And Rosalie Dene! How *do* your generation do it? Here you are, to my certain knowledge at least thirty-three and you don't look a day over *twenty*-three! My lamb, I'm so glad to see you after all this time! By the way, if that squeal I heard just now means that you think car thieves have gone off with the car, you're wrong. I drove her round to the garage. And while I think of it, do you always run things as fine? There wasn't a drop of petrol left in the tank. I handed her over to a man I found there and asked him to fill her up and have her ready for the road. I want to borrow her, Hilda."

"Of course you may. Come along in, though, it's much too cold to be standing here——"

"Isn't it?" Lady Russell gave a shiver. "I've got tea and

a glorious fire waiting for you in the study. I expect you can do with both after that long drive from Cardiff and your lengthy session with Commander Christy to follow."

She led the way to the study, a hand tucked through an arm of each. The room was rosy with the light of a roaring log fire. A laden tea-table had been drawn to one side of it and the big electric kettle was steaming comfortably.

"Shut the door, Rosalie, and drop your things over there," the Head said. "I don't know about you, but I'm cold and famished and I don't move from here till I've had my tea."

"I could do with mine, too," Rosalie agreed, tossing off coat and beret. "What a gorgeous fire! There's nothing like wood for a really hot fire."

Lady Russell looked up from her teapot. "I quite agree. Our living-room in Canada is the only one with an open grate, and though the house is summer-warm with the central heating, we tend to spend most of our free time in the living-room."

"Have you come alone or is Sir Jem with you?" Rosalie asked as she pulled up a humpty and sat down.

"Oh, he came, of course. Jack can carry on for him for the moment."

"And did you bring anyone else?" the Head asked eagerly.

Madge Russell chuckled. "Meaning the twins? Yes; they're here. Jo will have quite enough to do with her own babies and keeping an eye on the rest of the family, and my two are at the awful stage when they're just beginning to find their feet and you have to be after them the whole time. We're at Jo's house—Cartref—for the present."

She handed cups of steaming tea and a plate piled high with buttered toast.

"Where are your twins now?" Miss Annersley asked as she set to. "They're not over here, of course."

"They're at Cartref. I came alone. You can come over and see them whenever you like after this week, though. I think you will like them—they're really very nice."

"But why are you here at all?" Rosalie queried thoughtlessly.

Madge's face lost its laughter. "My dear girl, do you think I could stay away from Dick—my own twin—when he is in such trouble over Mollie?"

Rosalie reddened. "I'm sorry. That was stupid of me. Of course you would come. Have you been there yet?"

"No; we only arrived this morning and Jem thought we'd better settle into the house today and I come over for the car."

"Take it and welcome, my dear! Keep it as long as you want it. If we need one, we have the big one. Are you sure you wouldn't rather have that, by the way?"

"No; the runabout will do. You might need the big one for dental visits and so on. Thank you, Hilda."

"Madge—is it very—bad?" Miss Annersley spoke with fear in her voice.

Madge shook her head. "We can't say until we hear what Grafton Mann thinks. Dick was on the Transatlantic 'phone to us last Wednesday and he said then that their doctor is afraid it'll mean an op. It wouldn't matter so much if only her heart wasn't so dicky. Mercifully, they can do wonderful things nowadays in the way of counteracting post-operative shock, so we're all hoping that if it does come to that, it'll be all right. There's just this I can say. If it has to be done, it'll be kill or cure; but it means that if it was left, she wouldn't have a chance. They've tried to reduce the goitre with injections and medicines, but she hasn't responded."

"I knew that," Hilda Annersley replied. "Dick told me that their doctor's treatment hadn't done any good when he rang up to say they wanted Bride at home. She had planned to spend the half-term with Elfie, you see. I'm glad you've come, Madge. He has the children, of course; but even Peggy and Rix aren't eighteen yet. Peggy's at home, by the way. Did you know?"

Madge nodded.

"Does Dick know you're here?" the Head asked.

"No; we thought it better to say nothing in case it wasn't good flying weather. We couldn't have risked the twins if it hadn't been and I couldn't have left them yet. Jem told him that *he* would be arriving, though. In fact, I left him

110

trying to get through on the 'phone to announce his presence in England. I've left it to him whether he tells Dick I've come or not. Now that's enough about that. We truly can't say any more until Grafton Mann has made his examination. Let's change the subject. Do you realise you've never asked about Joey yet? Don't you want to know; or have you lost all interest in the creature?"

"Is it likely?" Hilda Annersley followed the lead at once. "We had Jack here just before term began, but he didn't give us much idea of the new arrivals. Most men are hopeless when it comes to wee babies. You tell us about them. Who are they like?"

"Nobody but themselves, so far. They're both very fair and they're lovely babies. Honestly, though, I can't see any family resemblance to anyone on either side. Jem says they must be a throwback to some distant ancestor."

"Are they good babies, Lady Russell?" asked Rosalie.

"Baby angels, so far." Madge spoke with caution. "They only yell at such times as any properly constituted baby would, and spend most of their time sleeping at present. Jo says most of the time she doesn't know she has twins! And that's as well. Mike's a perfect demon now that he can run all over. I want Jo to send him to a nursery school after Christmas. She says she won't, but she may change her tune when the twins start teething. The only time that boy is good is when he's asleep."

"And Jo herself?"

"Just herself—as wicked as ever, and not a day older than when she first married if looks are anything to go by! She had to do as she was told when she was with the nuns. They're dears, but martinets! But now she's back at home, it's another story. Luckily, she does pay attention to Jack, and he sees to it that she doesn't try to overdo things. And Canada has done her a world of good. I was horrified when she first arrived. She was all eyes and as white as chalk However, that's all over now. She's even beginning to grow *fat*!"

The other two shrieked at this, so she modified it a little.

"Well, perhaps that's rather strong. Let's say chubby. It suits her, you know. By the way, when I told her I was

111

coming, she spent nearly a whole day at her typewriter and the result is over there on your desk, Hilda. You can read it at your leisure. Now tell me all the news about school."

"I'll clear the crocks," Rosalie said, jumping up. "You won't be going back yet, will you?"

Madge looked at her watch. "I can give you another half-hour. I must catch the last ferry, though. I want to find out what Jem has arranged, and apart from that, I can't wish Kevin and Kester on to Marie for a whole night without warning."

Rosalie paused in her work for a moment to ask with real curiosity, "And who are *they* like?"

"Well, both have Jem's features, but Kevin is dark and Kester is fair, so we can't make any mistakes as to who is which. They're a jolly pair—always chuckling and cheerful. As to teething, I've had only one bad night up to date. Otherwise, we've only known it was happening when we found the teeth there. I just hope Jo has as good a time with her pair. She's had a benefit with Steve and Mike at one time and another, as you may remember."

Rosalie laughed, finished her job and wheeled the trolley out. They heard her speaking to someone in the hall. Then the door opened again and Matron appeared. Madge jumped up and flung her arms round her.

"Matey, how lovely to see you again! Oh, how under the sun have I kept away from you all so long? Come and sit down. Hilda is just going to tell me all the school news and you can help to jog her memory. Have you had a good week-end, by the way?"

"Very good, thank you," Matron said. "I suppose you've come across on Mrs. Bettany's account? How is she now?"

Madge nodded, gravity once more coming into her charming face. Matron gave her a sharp look but said nothing more, though her question went unanswered. All the senior members of the Staff knew that Mollie Bettany was suffering from Graves' disease and that a very serious operation was probably necessary. No good could be done by talking about it. They must just wait and hear what the great throat specialist had to say. Matron went to take off

112

her hat and coat and change her shoes. Then she ran down to the study and, for the next half-hour, Madge Russell listened eagerly to all the school news they could cram in in the time. She stood up at last.

"Well, even with the car, I must be off or I shall miss that ferry and then we'll have had it all round. I'll give you a ring as soon as we know anything, Hilda. Bride will be coming back tomorrow, I suppose; she will give you the latest up to then. I know Dick is taking Mollie to London the next day. I'll stay a day or two at the Quadrant—probably until the end of the week, so don't come over to Cartref to find us for we shan't be there. Grafton Mann may want to keep Mollie in town and perform the op. as soon as possible. I'll let you know when we're coming back."

"Yes, do. And mind you let us have all the news. We couldn't ring up ourselves and worry poor Dick, so it'll be a relief to have you there. Give him our love and Mollie, too, and tell them our thoughts and prayers are with them," the Head said.

Madge nodded. "Thank you, my dear. I don't expect I shall be away longer than that. I can't stay over here very long, you know. For one thing, Jo is supposed to be going to visit Lulu Redmond—I mean Lulu van Buren—in Vancouver Island and we don't want to leave it till too near Christmas. She's very well, but the change will do her good. She'll fly, of course, and take the twins, and I must be there to see to the rest. So it means only a few weeks here, at most. But oh, if—" She stopped short and said no more, but the other three could all finish the sentence for her.

If anything happened to Mollie Bettany, they knew that Madge would find it very hard to leave her twin brother in his distress.

"We can only leave it to God," Hilda Annersley said in her deep, beautiful voice. "And if He *should* take Dick's wife from him, he will still have their children, you know, and the twins and Bride are old enough to be very real comfort to him. But we must all pray that it may not happen."

113

Madge nodded. Then she ran out to the car, not trusting herself to speak.

"Poor Madge!" Hilda Annersley said as it disappeared round the end of the holly hedge.

"Poor Bride!" Matron remarked, her thoughts characteristically with the girl who was one of her charges.

"Poor all of them!" Rosalie added. "However, things won't be so bad for Bride. She will have *one* consolation we never thought possible this term, at any rate."

Matron turned and stared at her after they had entered the house again and the door was shut behind them. "What are you talking about? *What* consolation?"

Rosalie shot a pleading glance at the Head, who nodded. "Yes; tell her, Rosalie. She'll have to know, anyhow, to get the extra bed ready."

"What on earth *is* all this?" Matron demanded "*What* extra bed?"

"We've had a letter from Mr. Woodward, though he talked it over with me when I was at home this week-end. A distant cousin has written to offer to come and keep house for him and Elfie is coming back to school tomorrow!"

CHAPTER XIV

ELFIE RETURNS

"I SAY! Look at the time! Bride's painfully late, isn't she?"

This was Primrose Day in the Prefects' room where those grandees had assembled when they returned from the half-term holiday. Loveday, finding that they had mostly come by the same ferry, had seized the moment to convene a special prefects' meeting in order to plan for the party they always gave for the Staff this term.

Loveday glanced at the clock on the mantelpiece—"Five minutes to six!" she exclaimed. "Why, she must have missed the five-thirty ferry! That's not like Bride!"

Nancy Chester frowned and exchanged glances with her cousin Julie Lucy, the youngest of the prefects. "I hope there's nothing wrong with Aunt Mollie," she said slowly. "I know they've been worried about her for some time now—ever since last Easter, in fact."

The girls turned startled looks on her.

"But she was here for the Pageant last term," Loveday protested. "She looked quite fit then. Don't you remember how she laughed when Tom really blew on that conch shell of hers and set that ancient steed Peggy and Dickie were riding to bolt along the beach?"

Lesley Pitt began to laugh. "How mad Bride was about that! She just raged at her mother. She said Peg and Dickie might have been killed, but Mrs. Bettany only laughed again and said she'd be ashamed if any daughter of hers couldn't handle a poor old rattlebones like that!"

The girls laughed as they remembered. Then Primrose turned to Nancy to ask very gravely, "She wasn't ill then, was she Nance?"

"She was, though. Only she's the kind that doesn't give in till she just can't help it. When we came back after the summer hols, Bride told me that her mother had been very poorly most of the time and it seemed to be getting worse instead of better."

"What is it, Nance? Do you know?" Lesley asked.

"Some form of goitre—rather bad, I heard Dad say."

There was silence for a moment. Then Tom asked the question most of them wanted to ask. "What exactly *is* goitre, anyway?"

"Something to do with the thyroid gland. It causes a swelling at one side or the other of the throat, usually outside; but sometimes it scarcely shows at all. That's the kind Aunt Mollie has."

"Hush!" Loveday spoke imperatively. "I hear someone coming. Don't let her think we've been talking about her."

"That's not Bride—not unless she's produced an extra pair of feet!" Madge Dawson remarked. "Two people are coming."

Two people it was, though when the door opened, the only one they saw was big, sturdy Bride. She looked much as usual, Loveday thought at first glance, and she was grinning widely. The next moment, she was forgotten, for a much smaller girl slipped round her—a girl with a pointed chin and wide blue eyes which gave her a kitten-like appearance. At sight of her, the prefects rose in a body.

"Elfie!"—Elfie Woodward! Have you come for a visit?"
—"Oy, Elf, old thing, where did you spring from?" This last was Tom who had been very chummy with Elfie, and as Tom roared her query to make herself heard above the rest, Bride slammed the door.

"If you make a row like that, we'll have the staff down on us," she said. "Hello, everyone! Had a decent time? What's all this gathering in aid of?" Surely you aren't having a prefects' meeting to welcome Elf?"

She sounded so very matter-of-fact and normal, that most of the girls leaped to the conclusion that her mother must be better. Loveday, however, realised by this time that Bride's gaiety was very much on the surface and though her lips smiled, her eyes were very sombre. Nancy and Primrose dimly felt the same thing, but just sufficiently to make them feel uneasy.

"There isn't anything much to do before Prayers," Loveday said, carefully ignoring what she had seen. "We thought it would be rather a good notion if we went into a huddle about the Staff party, seeing we haven't done a thing about it, so far. You two are just in time. You *are* a prefect, aren't you, Elf?"

Elfie nodded rather apologetically. "So the Abbess told me."

"She's Games pree," Bride put in as she came forward.

"I don't want to take it on," Elfie broke in hurriedly. "It's been Bride's job and it ought to stay her job; but the Abbess says I must do it as she wants Bride for Bank prefect."

"For *what*? Bank prefect? Never heard of the creature before? It's news to me all right. What's the Bank prefect?" Anne Webster protested.

By this time, Bride had seated herself between Nancy and Primrose by the simple means of pushing hard with her chair till they move apart to make room for her. She waved Elfie to the seat of honour on the Head Girl's left hand. "You go there; that's your proper place. This will do me fine. Oh, my dears, I'm to take charge of Bank, of all things. I *ask* you! You must give your bank money to me and I hand out the receipts and then take it along to Miss Dene who parks it in the safe. Any time you want extra pennies for anything, you come along to me—at least you give in your name at Friday tea-time as usual and collect the cash on Saturday. That part isn't changed."

Nancy's jaw dropped conspicuously. "Oh *lor'*! Are you the best they can do? Well, I suppose the Abbess does know what she's doing, though I'm bound to say this makes me doubt it for once."

"You wait!" Bride told her. "I'll deal with you later. Go on and sit down, Elf. Why are you waiting? Now then, everyone, what's been arranged for the entertainment of our kind preceptresses?"

"Nothing, so far," Julie Lucy said while Elfie blushingly took her seat beside Loveday. "We'd only met, so to speak. We give the party—we know that. We go on from there. How are we going to amuse them? Got any ideas?"

"Nary one? What about the rest of you?"

Everyone else seemed to be as blank as she was, though Loveday begged for suggestions. Someone proposed a Hallowe'en party, but that had been done two or three times and the girls had decided that they must be original this time or perish in the attempt!

"What about making it a paper games party?" Bess Herbert proposed.

She was promptly howled down.

"Too dull for words! If that's the best you can do, I'd let it alone!" Lesley said scathingly.

"O.K.! Propose something better yourself!" Bess retorted.

"Could we have a treasure hunt? We could each provide some tiny thing and it's the fun, not the prize that counts." This came from Rosalind Yolland.

"Of course we couldn't! You know as well as anyone

117

that we give it in Hall. How do you imagine we could hide things in Hall?" Tom Gay demanded scornfully.

Lesley Pitt, who had been scribbling absently on the paper before her, took the floor again. "I wonder—could we make it a Book evening?"

"As how?" Primrose asked.

"Well, ask them to come dressed up to represent the title of some book—no; *wait*!" as one or two began to point out that this was just another way of saying 'fancy dress' and that had been done to death. "Let me finish before you start. We'll dress up ourselves and give our titles to Loveday who can list them. As each mistress arrives, she must give a slip with her title on to Loveday to add to ours. Then they have to guess what everyone represents—them *and* us. We'll give two prizes for the two best lists and a booby for the worst. Will that do?"

Nancy was the first to speak. "It's an idea," she said. "Definitely an idea!"

"We'd have to ask them to keep their titles secret, of course," Julie added. "And oughtn't they to be fairly well-known books?"

"Oh, of course! It wouldn't be fair otherwise."

"Well, we can put that down for one thing," Loveday said in relieved tones. "It ought to keep them busy quite half the evening. Then we'll have supper and we can spin that out for about an hour, I hope. What shall we do with them for the rest of the time?"

"Why not just have country-dancing?" Madge suggested.

"We can if we can think of nothing better; but I'd like to wind up with something—er—*unique*. Can't any of you do better than that?" Loveday asked discontentedly. "Elfie—what about you? Haven't *you* any ideas?"

"We-ell—I was just wondering if we couldn't give them a—a sort of obstacle race," Elfie responded slowly.

"An obstacle race?" Tom's eyebrows shot up. "D'you mean set them bounding over the horse and swarming up the ropes and crawling through bottomless sacks? Because if so, I don't mind telling you I just *don't* see the Staff joining in that sort of thing. Can you see Mlle, for instance, doing a neat squirm through a sack when she's in full party regalia? If so, you've a stronger imagination than I have!"

"I don't mean anything of that sort at all!" Elfie retorted. "I said 'a *sort* of obstacle race,' and what I'm thinking about hasn't anything to do with gym."

"Then what *did* you mean?" inquired Tom, completely mystified.

"Well—what about pinching a pair of shoes or slippers from each of them and mixing them all well together in one of those huge washing-baskets Karen uses for carting the washing about in fine weather? Two of us would carry it in and dump the lot on the floor and leave 'em to find their own. We'd have to do the pinching *after* they'd arrived in Hall, of course," she added calmly. "They'd miss the things if we took them before and might guess what we were after."

At the vision thus conjured up, even Bride's gravity relaxed and she shouted with the rest. This promising beginning set their brains going, and they had a busy and joyful time, thinking out various forms of torture for the mistresses. One or two ideas had to be banned as not exactly the sort of thing you could do with the Staff, however decent they might be, though they noted them for later use with their own rank and file. Some were snorted at as too ordinary and Loveday was determined to make this the sort of party that would be long remembered by all who enjoyed it. They managed to evolve an obstacle race of the kind the Staff might be expected to accept without too much demur. Parts of it would mean taking liberties with the possessions of those ladies, but, as Nancy pointed out, all the old ones could be relied on to play up and the rest would follow suit.

"They won't want any one of us—Staff or pupils—to think they're a lot of Miss Prissy Prims," she said shrewdly.

"Oh, they'll all join in; they're all quite decent," Bride said. "Peggy Burnett, for instance, was no angel when she was here as a pupil. I've heard Auntie Jo say that more than once."

Most of the rest of the school was already assembled for Abendessen when the prefects reached Hall, so the school at large had little chance of knowing that Elfie had come back. Indeed, it was not until they were saying grace that Mary-Lou spied her and was so startled that it is to be feared her prayers were mere lip-service that evening.

A good many other people were in her condition, too, but they must wait to talk until the Head had finished the few words with which she usually welcomed them, Then they were free to tell everyone else that Elfie Woodward had returned. Poor Elfie felt as if she were surrounded by eyes and nothing *but* eyes!

Miss Annersley, looking down the room, saw her embarrassment and decided to put a stop to it. Elfie was crimson and she had sent away her soup almost untouched.

She turned to Biddy O'Ryan who sat next her. "Look at those little ninnies!" she said crossly. "I'm going to give them something else to think about or poor Elfie will go hungry!" She struck her handbell sharply and the girls fell silent as its 'Pr-r-ring!' rang out. Everyone turned to look at the Staff table where the Head had risen to her feet. The startled maids stood where they were with plates and spoons in their hands, wondering why Miss Annersley should want to address the room just then.

"One moment, girls!" The Head's lovely voice carried to the farthest end of the room and everyone listened eagerly to what she had to say. "I see you all know that Elfie Woodward is now able to come back to school and continue her work. She will also be Games prefect as she would have been from the beginning if home circumstances had not kept her there until today. Bride has carried on for her very successfully, but now Elfie will take up her own job and Bride will take over a new post—that of Bank prefect. From now on if you require any extra money from Bank, you must hand in your names to Bride on the Friday evening and be ready to go to her in the prefects' room at nine next morning. Bank will open then and close at ten sharp. Remember this, please, for if you are later, you must do without your money until the next week. One thing more. I have the Christmas play now, and on Saturday you will be given your parts. It is a bigger thing than usual and will need a good many rehearsals, so as soon as you are given the parts, you must learn them. Now that is all. We will go on with our meal."

She sat down again and in the momentary silence that followed, a dull thumping was heard. At the same time, Prudence Dawbarn was seen to jump to her feet suddenly. Miss Annersley saw her and called her to order at once. Prudence was famed for being the most heedless young thing the school had ever harboured.

"Prudence! What are you doing, child? Sit down at once."

Far from sitting down, Prudence hurried up to the Staff table. "Please, Miss Annersley," she said excitedly, "Emerence Hope isn't here!"

"Not here? What do you mean?" the Head asked sharply. "Of course she is here; she came with Mary-Lou and Clem and Carola."

"Oh, I know *that*!" Prudence gasped, "but she isn't *here*—not here in the dining-room, I mean."

Miss Annersley cast a sweeping glance round the room, but nowhere could she see the gleaming fair hair and cheeky little face of Emerence. She turned her gaze back on Prudence and regarded her thoughtfully. Prudence wriggled uncomfortably and went red.

"Have you any idea where she is likely to be?"

Prudence's head drooped and she said in a queer, half-choked whisper, "Oh, p-please, I think she's—she's in the prefects' room."

Such of the prefects as could hear her literally sat up and looked at each other. What, oh *what* had that wretched Australian child been up to now?

Meanwhile, the Head was questioning Prudence. "In the prefects' room? *Emerence?* What do you mean, Prudence?"

"Please—I just think she's there and—and has got shut in."

There was a silence and now everyone could hear the thumps and bangs from upstairs.

"Run upstairs and see, will you, dear?" the Head said to Biddy O'Ryan.

Biddy was off, to return a minute later, her eyes like

121

two blue saucers. "Yes; she's there, but the room is locked and I rather think she's in one of the cupboards. Her voice sounded—muffled," she said shakily; the fact being that she was nearly suffocated with suppressed laughter.

Miss Annersley turned to a distant table where Loveday sat, keeping Upper III A in order. She was not near enough to have heard Prudence's information of Emerence's probable whereabouts, so was quite unperturbed as yet.

"Loveday, did you lock the door of the prefects' room when you came down?" the Head asked in impassive tones.

Loveday stood up with a startled look. She had heard the thuds like everyone else, but had passed it over as 'Some of the maids doing some hammering.' "Yes, Miss Annersley," she said. "I have the key here."

"Will you let me have it, please."

Loveday carried it over and Miss Annersley handed it to Miss O'Ryan who hurried off again.

Meanwhile, Miss O'Ryan had returned to the dining-room—though not with Emerence. She handed the key over to Matron, and went on with her meal.

Prayers followed at once and after that the Middles had to go to bed with their curiosity still unsatisfied. But next morning it came out that Emerence Hope had bet Prudence Dawbarn that she would hide in the prefects' room while they were having their meeting and get away with it safely. Unfortunately for Emerence, she had not bargained for falling asleep in the stuffy cupboard where she had hidden herself just before the grandees of the school had met. She had roused when Loveday had shut and locked the door behind her. At first, natural caution had kept her quiet; but when time went on and no one came, she began to think that she must stay where she was all night and that was more than she could bear. So she had shouted and thumped, at first with no result. Indeed, she was just beginning to resign herself to having to wait till next morning when she heard the handle of the door being turned. Then the door was shaken and after that came Miss O'Ryan's pretty Irish voice, demanding to know if she was there.

Freedom came very soon after that, but instead of being allowed to go down to the dining-room for Abendessen as she had expected, she was escorted to the study and told to wait there until Miss Annersley came. By that time, she was also beginning to realise that there was going to be trouble, so she sat down meekly and wished with all her might that she had never had that idea. It had seemed such a bright one when she got it, and all that had come of it was an uncomfortable nap from which she had roused with a slight headache, a good fright, for the prospect of a night in a cupboard had been very unpleasant, and now a row.

"And I'm *so* hungry!" thought Emerence woefully.

That part of it did not last long, for one of the maids arrived with her kedgeree and plate of prunes and custard and by the time she returned, the two plates were scraped clean. But half-an-hour after she had been set free, the Head arrived, looking very grave, and Emerence stood up, rubbing one foot up and down the other leg, and wished herself anywhere else.

When she heard her fate, she wished it even harder. All the Head said was that her sin was against the prefects, so they would deal with her on the morrow. Meantime, would she please understand that unless she was sent there for a definite reason, the prefects' room was forbidden ground to her.

She was then packed off to bed, by which time everyone else in her dormitory was safely in bed and presumably, asleep. It would not have done her much good if they had been awake, for Matron was there, waiting for her, and saw her into bed in a grim silence that made matters even more unpleasant.

It is hardly to be wondered at that when she was alone, Emerence burrowed under the clothes and wept at the thought of next day. Like most of her kind she would, on the whole, rather have fallen into the hands of the mistresses than the prefects!

CHAPTER XV

PARTY FOR THE STAFF

"IT really looks good, doesn't it? Whatever else happens, the Staff can't say we haven't done them proud in the matter of supper!" remarked Rosalind to Julie.

The fateful Friday had arrived and the prefects, all got up in a weird variety of costumes, were waiting for the arrival of their guests.

Julie's reply seemed to have little to do with the appetising-looking table. "Well, there's one thing: we've got clean cupboards in the prefects' room and I don't imagine Emerence or any of her gang will try to sneak into prefects' meetings again in a hurry."

The entire party broke into peals of laughter. They had been told by the Head that they must deal with Emerence and, after much argument, Lesley had been visited with an inspiration.

"She seems to like our cupboards. What's the matter with setting her to clean them out—*properly?*"

"In her own free time," Bride added dreamily. "*How* she'll love us!"

The idea had been duly carried out, despite wild protests from Emerence, who found herself condemned to spending all her spare time on the job until it was done. It took her exactly six evenings, by which time the two big cupboards were spick and span and she felt that she never wanted to set foot inside that room again.

"It really was a wizard idea," Bride said with a broad grin. "Well, I seem to hear the sound of steps on the stairs, so we'd better draw the curtains and remove ourselves to the other end of the room."

Bride was herself again. Her mother had been operated on six days before, had come well through the operation and, though still very weak, was reported as gaining ground steadily. Her recovery would be very slow, but it would be complete recovery and both Bride and Peggy, her elder sister, were rather above themselves in consequence. Lady Russell had returned two days before and was coming to the prefects' party, having seen Peggy off to Switzerland again, and all was well.

The door opened and the first pair of guests appeared. Miss Slater was in white tennis kit and Biddy O'Ryan was got up in clerical garb complete with dog-collar and high silk hat. The prefects stared, for they could think of no book-title that would fit either of these visions, who greeted them cheerfully before they went to hand their slips to Julie.

Miss Annersley and Miss Dene were the next to appear and the girls protested, for they simply wore their pretty evening dresses and had made no effort to dress up at all.

"Aren't you in for it?" Bride asked anxiously.

"Of course we are; but we're one book between the two of us," the Head told her with dancing eyes. "Come along, Rosalie. We must go and deposit our slip."

All in all, the Staff had shown a good deal of ingenuity in their efforts. Miss Derwent wore a swirling scarlet curtain which swathed her from head to foot and proved an enigma to most of them. Miss Stephens wore her school skirt and jumper twisted to one side so that the vent came down the middle and her stockings had the seams turned almost to the front, while her hair was corkscrewed up anyhow on top of her head.

Nor were the girls far behind. Bride had borrowed everyone's dancing pumps and was literally hung with them. They were draped round her neck and waist; hung on cords to the edge of her skirt and she had even managed a crown of cardboard to which she had sewn three pairs of her small sister's pink and blue pumps, for which she had sent home.

Julie had got herself up in an aged black skirt belonging to a dance-dress of her mother, a shawl and a bonnet and carried an enormous mangoldwurzel.

The first part of the evening went with a swing, with people darting from one person to another, considering what the dress could possibly represent, and a good many of the guesses were wild in the extreme.

The prefects had decided that the guessing must finish when the bell rang for school Abendessen, so as soon as it was silent, Loveday clapped her hands, called, "Time's up!" and then asked everyone to sit down and correct her list. "And only the name on the slip handed in counts!" she added severely. "Nothing else will do, so it's no use asking."

Peals of laughter rang out. Everyone knew that on these occasions there were a good many pleas for something that was 'Practically the same thing.' Then they all settled down and Loveday, with the list Julie supplied her, proceeded to read out.

"First, the Head and Miss Dene," she read impressively. "*Pillars of the House.*"

Everyone stared and gasped and then more shrieks of mirth came.

"Miss O'Ryan—*The Little Minister*," Loveday read. "Miss Stephens—*Oliver Twist*." She stopped looking bewildered.

Miss Stephens got up. "That is just what I am," she declared. "All over twist!"

Howls of indignation at this bare-faced pun greeted her announcement, but they were speedily hushed when Loveday, having recovered from the shock, held up her hand and read the next title. "Miss Slater—*The Woman in White*."

Most of the Staff had guessed this, but Peggy Burnett, who had appeared in a summer frock with an enormous question mark stitched on both back and front and proved to be as puzzling as Miss Annersley and Miss Dene. She now stood revealed as *Whose Body?* by Dorothy Sayers.

Reading out that list took some time and the rank and file of the school, returning from Abendessen, heard with feelings of envy the shouts and laughter proceeding from Hall.

Eventually, when lists had been all corrected, Loveday was able to announce that the first prize went to Miss Dene and the second to Miss Stephens, while Matron had won the booby.

"It's more than you deserve," Miss Derwent told her colleague crushingly, "perpetrating an appalling pun like that!"

Supper followed and was thoroughly enjoyed by everyone. The girls had done it all themselves and, as the Head remarked to Frau Mieders, were a credit to their domestic science training.

"I wonder what they mean to do with us after supper?" Lady Russell murmured to Mlle de Lachennais who sat beside her.

"Dance, perhaps?" Mlle suggested.

"No-o, I don't think so. Some of those young monkeys are nearly bursting with some mighty secret and I don't think it had anything to do with dancing."

She proved right. For, just then, Loveday stood up and announced the Obstacle Race.

"It's a different kind of obstacle race," she explained after sundry protests at anything so violent after the big meal they had all eaten had died away. "We don't ask you to do anything very athletic. Here come Tom and Bride with the first obstacle."

The big doors opened at the end and Bride and Tom stalked in carrying an enormous washing-basket, closely covered with a sheet between them. They set it down carefully in the middle of the floor and then stood back and eyed Loveday expectantly.

The Head Girl cleared her throat and then announced in a rather higher key than usual, "Er—this basket contains one pair of shoes belonging to each of you. We—we borrowed them a short while ago and—er—hope you don't mind. The basket will be turned out and you must each find your own shoes and put them on. The first to do so has won the first obstacle."

"What impudence!" Lady Russell exclaimed, laughing. "But what are you doing about *me*?"

"That's O.K.," Bride informed her unexpectedly. "I pinched a pair of yours when I came over yesterday with that message from Dad. It came in awfully usefully!"

127

Her aunt collapsed and Hall rang with laughter. Tom and Bride turned to their basket, whipped off the sheet and then turned it upside down, effectually dumping the shoes in every direction. Indeed, the well-waxed floor sent one of Mlle.'s dainty walking-shoes sliding right up to her and she picked it up with a cry of delight.

After that the Staff pounced on the main heap with cries and exclamations and there was a regular scramble for the next two or three minutes. Miss Burnett was first. Bride had not noticed that her name was printed on wide white tape which had been sewn under the tongue of each of her stout walking-shoes. It was an easy matter for her to swoop down on such as looked about her size, turn back the tongues and find her own. She hurriedly changed and then raced to Loveday for the second obstacle.

"Just a moment," Loveday said. "Put her name down, Bess."

Bess scribbled it down and sat waiting. Mlle came second. Then half-a-dozen people proclaimed that they had their own shoes and the rest came after.

The next obstacle had been evolved by Julie. Every mistress was handed a sheaf of papers and envelopes all written on, and informed that each page had its own envelope and they must match them up, fold the paper and put it in its proper envelope.

Miss Dene scored here. She had her dozen envelopes filled in next to no time, and had handed them over while most of her colleagues were trying to decide on the third or fourth of theirs.

Suddenly, a wild splutter from Biddy O'Ryan made them all turn to see what was amusing her. She held out the sheet proclaiming, "It's not fair at all, at all! Why should *my* sins be remembered like this?"

Bride, with a memory of the tales she had heard from her Aunt Jo had scribbled on the paper, "What price sleeping in Bill's bedroom?" a recollection of Biddy's punishment in Tirol days for scaring all her dormitory with hair-raising yarns about banshees.

She managed to come second, though, and presently all the sheets and envelopes had been matched up and handed back and the Staff were ready for their third obstacle.

This time, each was handed a very neat parcel and requested to open it and find the owners of its contents and hand them back. Puzzled, the Staff obeyed, and found themselves gazing amazedly at well-laundered underthings and handkerchiefs.

"You imps!" Lady Russell exclaimed. "Have you been rifling everyone's drawers?"

"Oh, *no!*" came a shocked chorus.

Nancy Chester added quickly, "We wouldn't *dream* of doing a thing like that! We only took them from the laundry."

"I did have a go at *your* drawers," Bride informed her aunt. "That didn't count and I knew you wouldn't mind. Now will you all get cracking, please."

This was not nearly so difficult as some of the others had been. Everyone's garments were well and truly marked and it was just a question of finding the marks and returning the things to their owners. The girls had been very careful not to rumple anything and the Staff were equally careful. At least five people finished at one and the same moment and only Frau Mieders was left out of the next shout of "Finished!" She had one garment which seemed to be unmarked and was unable to find an owner for it.

The Staff clustered round her examining it and mostly denying it. Then Miss Oldroyd, the young and rather shy Junior English mistress gave an exclamation, turned it inside out—it was a slip—and pointed to a neat 'C.V.O.' printed down one of the seams.

"I always try to mark so that it isn't too obvious," she explained.

"I should say you succeeded," Lady Russell said, laughing. "Well, what new torment have you young wretches for us next?"

The curtains shrouding the supper table were drawn back by Audrey, Bess and Primrose, who had disappeared during the last obstacle, and showed that the table had been cleared—the guests had heard this going on and thought how very considerate the girls were!—and in place of the dishes, plates and glasses, there were now

129

thirteen photographs strewn about, all of babies at different stages.

"These," said Lesley who was in charge of it, "are all photos of us when we were babies. Will you please fit the right photo to the right person? Here are the slips for it." She produced a bunch of slips and gave them out. Then the Staff crowded round the photos which were mainly snaps and took a gentle revenge for the indignities they had suffered by commenting freely on the subjects.

"Well," Miss Burnett remarked as she surveyed one of a yawning infant which seemed to be mainly mouth, "who on earth has a mouth like a slit in a pillar-box?" She peered round at the girls, who grinned back at her.

"You *all* have!" she decided. "Do stop grinning like that! You remind me of a cluster of cannibals choosing the latest victim for the cooking-pot!"

"Lady Russell will be able to spot Bride on sight," Biddy O'Ryan sighed.

Bride chuckled at this. She was very sure that her aunt would *not* recognise her, for she had found an old snap of herself at six weeks. Either she or the camera must have moved, for she appeared with double lines, and she defied anyone to know it for herself.

Suddenly, she was seized from behind and Mlle de Lachennais was pushing back her hair to examine her ears.

"The ear," little Mlle explained placidly, "does not alter shape, so we may guess by it who those two showing the baby lying on its side has become. No, Bride, it is not of you. I must see someone else."

The Staff declared that this was the worst of the obstacles, so far. The girls gave them twenty minutes for it and then insisted that time was up and collected the papers, most of which showed a sadly blank appearance.

Primrose presided over the next effort. She produced a basket of small apples which everyone recognised with protests. They were very pretty apples, yellowish green with a rosy cheek, but they were so tart that it was impossible to eat them raw, and Karen after two or three attempts at cooking them, had given it up in disgust. Stew as long or as carefully as she might, they remained hard.

"What are you doing with those?" the Head demanded.

Primrose solemnly offered her basket, requesting each mistress to take one. One prefect moved in front of each member of the Staff and produced her watch and Primrose explained.

"You try to eat your apple," she said blandly. "The one who manages to eat most without making a face wins. You stop if you make a face, though."

"And I flattered myself you felt some affection for us!" Lady Russell groaned. "Oh, well, here goes!"

She shut her eyes, bit into the apple and chewed—for one second. The next moment she had produced her handkerchief and removed the mouthful with a shudder.

"Urrh! What horrible things! My mouth's all dry!"

Most of the rest followed her example—all except Miss Armitage, the new science mistress. So far she had remained something of a dark horse to both girls and mistresses. Now, she established herself so far as the girls, at any rate, were concerned. She munched away at her apple, swallowing mouthful after mouthful stolidly while the others watched her, nearly open-mouthed.

"Well!" Miss Stephens gasped as her colleague dropped the core on to the dish provided and wiped her fingers on her handkerchief. "What's your mouth made of inside —corrugated iron?"

Miss Armitage gave her a solemn grin and then explained. "We have a tree of the same sort at home. I'm the only girl with five brothers. I learnt to do a lot of things without squirming."

"Well, you win that event, anyhow," Primrose said briskly. "None of the others got through even *one* mouthful."

"Is that the end?" Lady Russell asked plaintively.

"No; there's just one more. We play a game of Follow-my-Leader and if you can't do anything the Leader does, you drop out. The one who stays in longest wins. Tom is Leader!" Loveday said this sweetly and a concerted groan arose from the Staff.

"None of us will last very long at that rate!" Miss Stephens declared.

"I'll let you down lightly at first," Tom said reassuringly as she went to the head of the line that had formed. "Besides, *we're* all joining in this—except Bride. She's got to play. Go ahead, Bride!"

Bride struck up a lively march and Tom led off. They marched round Hall, then they hopped for a dozen yards. Then they went in a very jerky fashion, for at every fifth step Tom sat down on the nearest chair and her followers had to do the same. This was all easy enough. But when she did "Knees bend!" and they all had to proceed by jumps, first Frau Mieders and then Miss Denny gave out. The rest contrived to stick it out; but her next effort finished Madge Russell, Miss Slater, Mlle and Miss Lawrence. It consisted in setting one foot on the seat of every other chair and, as Miss Slater said breathlessly when she sat down, they had had a sufficiently athletic doing before that!

But the next business left only Biddy O'Ryan and Peggy Burnett of the mistresses, for Tom lay down full length and *rolled* over and over for at least ten feet. Then, with an eye on the clock, she decided to finish it—which she did with a series of handsprings that defeated Peggy, who knew that her ankle would not stand much of *that* and the history mistress was left the winner.

Finally, the marks the girls had awarded were added up and after some consideration, it was found that Biddy had won by two marks, Rosalie Dene coming second.

The prizes, two large boxes of chocolates, were awarded and then the Head, who had also kept her eye on the clock, stood up.

"This has been a memorable evening," she said solemnly. "Thank you very much, girls. And now, as it's a quarter to eleven, I think that we must say good-bye—or rather, good-night."

"We *must* have The Queen!" Bride cried, plunging towards the piano.

Miss Lawrence was before her. She struck the chord and everyone sang 'God Save the Queen' with all the energy left in them.

CHAPTER XVI

A CHAPTER OF TROUBLES

AFTER that particular break, Staff and prefects settled down to hard work. A good many of the elder girls had public exams to face at the end of the year. Most of them hoped for a final year at the new branch the school had opened in Switzerland, but their parents had informed them that this would depend on what their work this year was like. As no one wanted to be left out of that adventure if it could be avoided, it proved a useful incentive to steady work.

So far as the rest were concerned, there was the Christmas play and it was an understood thing that any girl who got into serious trouble would be turned out of it. That was a disgrace that had seldom or never occurred.

Emerence, especially, having never had the chance to be in any sort of play before, had made up her mind to be as good as she could. She had a small speaking part and she felt that if anything happened to cause her to lose it, she would die of grief on the spot!

One evening, about a week after the prefects' party, Mlle, who had been sitting quietly marking Lower IV A's French, suddenly heaved a sigh so deep it was almost a groan.

"Anything wrong?" Miss Derwent asked, looking up from Upper Fifth's précis work. "You sound as if you had toothache."

"Mais non," Mlle replied. "But tell me, do you have anything to do with Lower IV A?"

"No, thank Heaven!" Miss Derwent spoke with emphasis. "I find Upper IV B quite as trying as I like. If I had to deal with those young demons in Lower— A *or* B —I should go ravers and you'd find me sitting on the floor sticking straws in my hair!"

"It is what I feel like now," Mlle sighed.

"What have they been up to?" Biddy O'Ryan asked.

Mlle poured forth her woes. "I gave them a short French composition to write. They have a picture in their text-book and they describe it to me—see!" She held out the book and the Staff, not sorry for a short rest from their work, crowded round.

It was a simple picture of a farmyard, gaily coloured and showing among other things poultry, a cow, some sheep, a haystack and a sheepdog. There was plenty for even people like Lower IV to manage eight or ten short sentences without straining themselves too much, Mlle, however, dropped the book and waved her hand towards the exercise-books lying about her table. One and all were heavily marked and lined in red ink and, to judge by what they saw, the Staff guessed that there would be a heavy detention roll next day.

"What have the little ninnies been doing?" Biddy demanded.

Mlle fished out Priscilla's book and showed that the beginning of practically every sentence was crossed through. "That child! She has begun almost each sentence with 'voilà' and I have spent three lessons—but *three*," she spoke impressively, "explaining that 'voilà' is used when you point to something and in this case it should have been 'Il y a'."

"But have they *all* done that?" Biddy asked.

"Oh, no; that is only Priscilla. But Frances Wilford has not once remembered to make her adjectives agree in gender and number with their nouns; and Emerence Hope has *invented* words—and such words!"

"*What* words? Oh do let us see!" Peggy implored.

For answer, Mlle held out the book and the delighted Staff read: 'C'est un tableau d'un cour de la ferme. Il y a une taurelle à la porte, et trois moutons bianca. Un mouton-chien——'

At this point, Biddy O'Ryan let herself go and shouted with laughter. "Oh—*oh!* "Un mouton-chien!" Where on earth *did* she get that?"

"Mais j'en ai dit. C'est une invention!" Mlle replied rather indignantly.

134

"What else has she said? This is rich! I must copy it for Jo—she'll love it!" And Biddy reached over to her table for paper and pencil and calmly copied out Emerence's exercise, pausing to chuckle over such weird inventions as 'une elle-coq' for hen; 'un foin-colline' for haystack and, finally, 'Un grand chacal est dans l'étable.'

"A jackal in the stable?" Miss Derwent said, puzzled. Then she saw and went off into fits of laughter. "She means 'un cheval'!"

The Staff room rang with their merriment and Mlle, who had at first looked indignant, was forced to join in. Certainly, if Emerence had intended to give them a little amusement, she had succeeded!

As she had intended nothing of the kind, she was righteously annoyed when next day Mlle told her among other things that the exercise must be rewritten; every word she did not know to be copied out in a notebook which was given her, and all the words to be learnt by heart and repeated to the mistress at some later and unspecified date.

Emerence had to copy them into her notebook and then use up some of her precious free time in learning them. It took every moment of prep for her to get through her daily work, for she had no wish to be put down, so her only chance was to work at them while the others were amusing themselves. She was very sulky for the next day or two. It seemed to her that she was *always* having to give up her spare time to things she did not like!

She had been amazingly good for her, after the first outbursts, but no one can hope to reform in six or seven weeks unless they are saints and Emerence was no saint. When three days later she was told sharply by Miss Stephens that if she did not do better work in geography she would be sent down to Lower III for that lesson, she felt ready to fight with her own shadow.

It was unlucky that Mary-Lou, knowing nothing of all that, since she was in the form above, should have taken it upon herself to make remarks about Emerence's netball. At first the new girl had taken very kindly to the game and she had made rapid strides in her form. That day Emerence had made almost every possible mistake she could during that afternoon's practice and finally lost her temper and started a slanging match with Priscilla Waw-barn, which had so incensed Julie Lucy who was taking the practice, that she had sent the pair of them off the field with the remark that if they couldn't behave better than that, they had best keep away altogether!

Mary-Lou had been chosen captain of the Junior Middles' team and had been considering Emerence for a reserve, so she was grievously upset by the afternoon's events and when the pair of them met in their common room, she told Emerence exactly what she thought of her. Emerence flared up and retorted as rudely as she could and finally ended up with swearing at Mary-Lou, which so horrified the rest, that they proceeded to send her to Coventry and told her that they would have nothing to do with her until she had apologised to Mary-Lou for saying what she had done.

Emerence regarded them with an impudent smile, "Oh, that's nothing to what I *could* say!" she told them.

As the bell rang for prep just then, they all had to go; but when Abendessen came, Emerence found that she was to be left severely to herself. They saw that she had everything she needed, but further than that, no one would go; and when she addressed a remark to Ruth Barnes, she first stared at her as freezingly as she could and then said, "We're not talking to you!" with such finality that Emerence said no more.

She thought of it, however; and during the rest of the evening when all the others were busy with games, jigsaw puzzles and chatter, she sat alone in a corner of the room and was utterly miserable.

The next day Commander Christy, having done all that he could do about the tunnel for the present and seen that the bridge across the brook was well railed on both sides, had the wire fencing removed and told the Head that there was no reason why the girls shouldn't go there now. It was safe enough and even the pond was nowhere deeper than four feet and that was in the centre.

Miss Annersley agreed and the school was told that the embargo was lifted and they might go and see the latest addition to their grounds. The only restriction was that all below Upper IV B must have a mistress or a Senior with them at present. Apart from that they were free to go in their spare time.

For the first two or three days, it proved a magnet to even the prefects. After that, they were more or less used to it.

Emerence, still largely ignored by her own gang, had gone with the rest when Miss O'Ryan had taken them for their morning walk that way. The pond appealed to her and she was moved to ask of Miss O'Ryan how it was that the pond never overflowed. Biddy O'Ryan was a kindly creature and she had seen the miserable look on the little Australian's face. She saw nothing to worry about in Emerence's question and she explained about the outfall at the farther end of the pond and even went so far as to take the girls and show them where the water ran into the big ditch in the lane.

"What would happen if this end got choked up, Miss O'Ryan?" Vi Lucy asked curiously.

"Well, I suppose eventually the pond would overflow and we'd have a flood," Biddy said, laughing. "Let's hope it doesn't happen. It would mean going to the playing field by the school gardens and that's a long round to have to take—especially when you're tired after a stiff match at hockey or laxe—or even netball. Well, I think you've seen everything there is to see now and we must go on."

They marched briskly away and no one thought any more about it. Vi's question had been a more or less idle one and at least half the others hadn't bothered much about the answer.

Emerence, however, had taken it all in. She had had previous experience which they had not. Moreover, she was in a queer state at present and she was very resentful about the way she was being treated. It was a pity, as it turned out, that no one made any advances to her that day. If they had, she might have come out of her sulks, and then what the rest of the Junior Middles spoke of as long as they were at school, as "the great row," might not have happened.

The day had begun with blue skies and a bright sun; but as it went on the sun departed and the skies turned grey, and by the time Lower IV A left the art room (where Emerence had tried Herr Laubach, the art master, to such a pitch that he finally turned her out of the class) and went to prep in their own form room, a fine, misty rain was falling.

It was also an unhappy coincidence that this prep was taken by Julie Lucy, who had been looking forward to a good netball practice with the team in preparation for their match against St. Ronan's School on Saturday afternoon. Julie was cross because the practice was definitely off, thanks to the rain, and her juniors realised it when she stalked into their form room, armed with her Livy, Latin grammar and dictionary, and wearing a black scowl. They glanced at each other warningly and for the first twenty minutes, prep went on in utter silence. Julie, buckling down to her Livy, felt thankful for it.

But small girls of thirteen can hardly be expected to remain quiet for ever and presently there were the usual rustlings and little sounds. Then Cherry Christy who had tied herself up in a knot over some arithmetic ventured to put up her hand. Julie, buried in her Latin, never noticed. Cherry sat for a minute which felt like five and then spoke.

"Please, Julie, I can't do this sum."

Julie looked up. "Bring it here," she said resignedly. "Where's your question?" she asked.

Cherry gave her the text-book. Julie read it over.

"But why have you tried to *divide?*" she asked.

Cherry wriggled and looked foolish. "I—I thought it *was* division," she said finally.

"Oh, Cherry! Look at it!" And Julie read: " 'If seven boxes of sweets cost £1 4s. 6d., what will be the cost of twenty-eight boxes?' "

"Well, but I had to find out what *one* box would cost," Cherry argued.

"No need—if you know your seven times table."

Cherry looked sulky. She hated arithmetic in any case and she had struggled with that wretched sum till she was in no case to think clearly. Julie waited a minute or two. Then she spoke again.

"Say the table—aloud," she ordered.

Cherry began it. "Seven ones are seven—seven twos are fourteen—seven threes are twenty-one—seven fours are twenty-eight——"

She was about to go on, but the prefect stopped her. "There's your twenty-eight! You are given the cost of seven boxes, so all you have to do is to multiply by four. Now trot back to your seat and go on."

Cherry went back, flushed and rebellious. Julie had made her feel like an idiot and she *still* had that sum to do.

Julie returned to her Livy, but the peace had been definitely broken now. The next to want something was Angela Carter who was nearly in tears because she couldn't find "he shall have" in her French vocabulary. Wondering if Lower IV A had lost their wits, the prefect set her right, and returned to her own work. Just then a slight scuffle at the back of the room made her jerk her head up sharply to see what was going on. Emerence Hope was leaning over from her desk, clutching one side of an exercise book while Priscilla Dawbarn held firmly on to the other. As Julie looked up, the unhappy book tore in half and they were left with half each.

Julie jumped up. She had been in a bad temper before, but this finished it.

"Stand up, you two!" she said curtly. "What are you doing? Come here at once and bring that book to me. The rest of you go on with your work. If you haven't any to do, you may go to your form mistress and tell her, and ask her to set you something more to keep you busy."

With at least two-thirds of their prep still to do, Lower IV A glued their eyes to what they were supposed to be doing and Julie began her inquiry.

"What—were—you—doing?" she repeated once more with a pause between each word.

"Please," Priscilla said, "I only wanted to know what the prep was for Latin."

"Why didn't you get it down at the lesson?"

"Miss Burnett sent for me for my foot remedials."

"Was it your own fault you had to go then?" Julie asked shrewdly.

On this occasion, however, Priscilla had a clear conscience. "No; it's my usual time," she explained, "but Miss Oldroyd went on a bit longer than usual so I had to go before she gave out the prep."

"I see." Julie was beginning to recover herself. "But why didn't you ask someone about it sooner? And in any case, why did you grab Emerence's book like that? And, as far as that goes, if you didn't know what it was, why didn't you do something else and ask later? You still have evening prep."

Priscilla had nothing to say to this.

Julie waited for an answer. Then, seeing that she would not get one without a good deal of fuss, she turned to Emerence. "Why couldn't you tell Priscilla what the prep was without making such a nuisance of yourself?" she demanded.

" 'Cos I didn't," Emerence muttered.

Julie looked at her. "Why not?"

Emerence was no telltale, whatever other faults she might have. She couldn't very well say that Priscilla, getting no response to her signals, had reached back and snatched the book, so she said nothing. Priscilla spoke up for herself.

"I—I suppose it was my fault," she said in a very humble tone. "I tried to bag it and she hung on to stop me."

"I think you've behaved like a pair of St. Agnes' babies!" the exasperated Julie said. "Well, you can just remain where you are for the rest of prep and make up what you miss now at the end of evening prep. As for the book, you must settle that with Miss Dene."

Gasps of dismay came from both the culprits. There were nearly twenty minutes left of prep; and Priscilla knew, if Emerence did not, just what Miss Dene would have to say about that torn book.

Unfortunately, Julie's treatment had put the finishing touches to Emerence's resentment. She was literally boiling by the time she had done that extra twenty minutes before

140

Abendessen and she must do something to relieve her feelings or burst! Julie herself was busy with other things, and once she had dismissed the pair, thought no more about it.

Priscilla went to bed and to sleep without worrying about what had happened. That sort of thing was very much in the day's work with her. Emerence, on the other hand, lay awake for nearly an hour, planning her revenge on *everyone!*

Next day, when the rain was still coming down and they could have no games in consequence, Emerence disappeared from her form room and was gone for half-an-hour. It was prep again, but no one was sitting with them as it happened. This occasionally occurred and they were on their honour to behave themselves. To their credit, be it said, they very rarely gave anyone reason to worry about it. As a whole, the Chalet School was proud that they could be trusted to behave, even if no one was with them. Of course, if they were under supervision, that was another matter—at any rate so far as the young Middles were concerned.

Funnily enough, no one thought anything about it at the time. Heather Clayton, who was form prefect, only thought Emerence must have gone for remedials, so nothing was said when she arrived half-an-hour after prep had begun. She looked brighter when she came in and she buried herself in her lessons and refused to look at anyone. Besides, they weren't "speaking" to her, though some of them were beginning to forget that they had a grievance and, if she had given them any chance, would have been as friendly as usual.

The rain cleared up through the night, but the hockey match had had to be called off, for the playing field was sodden. The netball court, being of *en-tout-cas*, was not affected.

After Frühstück, Julie went out with Rosalind Yolland and Pat Collins, two members of the school team, to inspect the court and make sure that everything was all right. They arrived back a quarter of an hour later, tearing over the ground at full speed and dashed to the study where they banged on the door with complete lack of ceremony. Ten minutes later, it was all over the school that something must have happened to the new pond, for it had flooded badly. So had the brook, and there was no getting near the bridge, since water lay all round it on either side for a distance of six or eight feet!

"And that means," Julie said disgustedly, "that we'll have to take the long way round both before and after the match. And that's a nice thing! nearly fifteen minutes' walk both ways! Oh, why on earth couldn't Burnie have kept off the well and leap elsewhere if leap she must?"

CHAPTER XII

A SHARP LESSON

THERE was nothing they could do about it then. Miss Annersley rang up Commander Christy, wishing as she did so that she had insisted at the very beginning that the well should be filled in again. It was too late to do anything about that just now, but she meant to have a serious talk with him on the subject at the earliest moment. This sort of thing was beyond a joke!

The owner of the property came over post-haste. Accompanied by the Head he walked across to see what had really happened. The brook, except for a long ripple down the centre of the wide-spreading lake, was not to be seen. The pond was nearly bank high and they could see for themselves that the flood was spreading. The little bridge was just, and only just, above the surface of the water and there was no going near it.

"I don't understand it at all," said Commander Christy. "The ditch was deepened and I'm certain there was nothing there to choke up the outflow. At the same time, choked it must be. We had better go and inspect it. This is going on, you know. We've had an abnormally wet autumn this year and I expect the spring is running very full. Shall we go?"

Miss Annersley resignedly accompanied him across the wet turf over the stile and down the lane to the spot where the original outflow had run into the ditch. The brickwork had carried on, as he informed her, sinking under the bed of the ditch, and he meant to have it all cleared as soon as he had found what lay at the other end. That, however, could not be done for the moment. In the meantime, the ditch should have been sufficient to carry off the overflow of the water from the pond.

Thanks to the rain, it was full without the pond-water, but as Michael Christy pointed out, the force of that, if it had been running, would have been enough to keep it going, for here the lane descended a gentle slope and the ditch ended in a duck pond in a field belonging to one of the tenant farmers. There was a further overflow at the far end of the duck pond, which in very wet weather sent a trickle of water over the cliff, so there was no danger of flooding normally.

The pair stooped down to see if they could see anything, but the full ditch made it impossible, for the mouth of the outflow lay below the edge of the path. Commander Christy grimaced, and then began to pull off his coat and roll up his shirt sleeves.

"What on earth are you going to do?" the Head demanded.

"Looking's no good. I'll have to feel—and a nice wet job it will be!" he retorted. "Hang on to these for me, Hilda. There doesn't seem to be anywhere I can lay them down."

By this time, he had also removed his shoes and socks. He handed her the socks and coat, rolled up his trousers, and with a renewed grimace for the chill of the water, splashed down into the ditch and began feeling round the mouth of the over-flow, the Head watching him anxiously from the lane.

Suddenly, he gave an exclamation and began to haul. "Got it! Though whether I can yank it out is another matter. It seems to be wedged, whatever it is."

The Head watched him anxiously as he tugged and pulled. At last, when she was beginning to shiver in the cold wind and her feet felt like ice with standing on the wet clay, he gave it up and scrambled out.

"It's no go! I'll have to have someone to help me and poles or a hook of some kind to free whatever it is. But this is no fair play, Hilda. That obstruction is firmly wedged and was shoved in by hands. Hilda, I'm going to bag that big man of yours. He's stronger than poor old Pugh and between us we ought to get that drain clear. You go and stay by the fire and keep warm."

Miss Annersley did as she was told, for she could see that she would be no help to the men.

It was nearly twelve o'clock before Commander Christy came up to the house, wet and cold, but triumphant.

"We've got it!" he announced.

"What was it?"

"An old scarecrow."

"What?"

"An old scarecrow. I rather think it was one that Owen had tossed out of his field last week. He told me he wanted to set up a new one as the present thing was dropping to pieces. He ought to have burnt it, of course; but I should think he told his man to dispose of it and the lazy beggar just shoved it over the hedge into the lane. It's at the corner where the wheatfield and that sheep pasture meet and I don't suppose he thought anything more about it."

"But how on earth did it get there?" Miss Annersley demanded.

Michael Christy looked rueful. "I knew you'd ask me that."

"Well, what else do you expect? If *you* had charge of several young demons who act before they think and are as full of mischief as a cageful of monkeys, you would want to know too? Have you any reason for thinking it was any of the girls?"

For reply, he produced a gym girdle, sodden and muddy, but still recognisable as a gym girdle. The Head took it and turned it over. There was a name-tape stitched to one end, but it was so smeared with mud that it was impossible to read the name. Matron took it from her, produced a small towel and wiped it thoroughly. Then she nodded.

"Just as I thought! Emerence Hope! If ever there was an imp of evil, it's that child. Well, Con Stewart warned us what she was like, so we can't be surprised. But what I want to know is what has she been doing about a girdle?"

"She probably has half-a-dozen of 'em," the Commander said. "Isn't that the kid whose folk are millionaires and who was allowed to run wild until they sent her here?"

"It is. Oh, dear! She really did seem to have settled down well and to be no worse than several others I could name. Well, I suppose I must have her in for questioning. Ring the bell for Rosalie, Matey, and let's get it over. Sit down, Michael, and warm yourself. You ought to be here, seeing you discovered this. Poor little soul!" The Head's voice was full of pity. "I wonder what made her do such a stupid thing?"

"Natural depravity, I imagine," Commander Christy said, sitting down. "Hilda, you sound *sorry* for the imp!"

"So I am. If her silly parents had only taught her to control herself when she was small, she would be the usual naughty girl, I expect, but no more. As it is, she has to suffer for their stupidity—Oh, Rosalie, go and ask whoever is taking Lower IV A to excuse Emerence, will you, and bring her here to me."

Rosalie went on her errand and Michael Christy, who had been staring at the Head with an amazed look, promptly asked, "Do you really blame her parents for this sort of mischief?"

"In the first instance—yes. They let her go her own way and now, when she has to come to order and meets unpleasantness, she can't take them and tries to pay back other folk for them. If she really is at the bottom of all this mess, I shall have to punish her, for she *must* learn that you can't go through life following your own sweet will, regardless of what happens to others. I don't like doing it, for I do feel that it's unfair to the child."

"Rot! She's not lacking is she? She knew well enough that it was an outrageous thing to do. If she were a boy I'd give her a good thrashing myself and that's what she deserves." Commander Christy had had to waste a whole morning over clearing the drain. He had been working up to his knees in a ditch filled with chilly rain water, to say nothing of all the work needed to get the scarecrow free, and he was in a thoroughly irritable mood.

"Oh yes; she would know it was wrong," Miss Annersley said calmly, "but I don't suppose she stopped to think of that. She's never been taught to think."

"Then a good caning would go a long way to teaching her, I should say!" he retorted huffily.

"No; it would only put her back up and make her feel that all her world was against her. That's a bad mood for a child of thirteen. I know you're furious, Michael. If it had been done by anyone like Mary-Lou Trelawney or, say, your own Dickie, I should agree that a good caning was probably the best thing for her. But Mary-Lou and Dickie have had sensible training all their lives. They have known proper control from the start. There would be no excuse for them. There *is* every excuse for a girl who has been allowed to grow up thinking she can do just as she likes. She won't escape punishment—you may be sure of that. But corporal punishment won't do her any good."

"Huh! Well, I suppose you know your own job best," he grunted. Then Rosalie appeared, bringing a scared-looking Emerence with her, and the conversation ceased.

Matron's eyes darted towards the girl's waist. Emerence was wearing a girdle, however, so nothing was to be gained from that.

"Come in, Emerence," the Head said. "Come here to me, child."

Emerence came. When she was standing beside Miss Annersley, that lady put a hand on the small thin shoulder nearest and said, "Tell me, Emerence, did you stop up the drain?"

Emerence always told the truth, whatever else she did, so she looked the Head in the face and blurted out, "Yes; I did."

"When?"

"Yesterday afternoon when we couldn't have games."

146

This gave Miss Annersley a jar. "But how did you manage it?" she exclaimed.

Emerence explained—rather defiantly, but she was feeling frightened now and defiance was the only way she knew of meeting it. "We didn't have anyone with us for prep so I just went out. The others didn't know. I think they thought I'd gone for remedials."

"I see. Now tell me, Emerence, why did you do such a stupid thing?"

Emerence was silent. When she did speak, it had nothing to do with the question. "Why did you guess it was me?"

"Commander Christy found your girdle."

"Mixed up with that old scarecrow you shoved in," he put in. He had been eyeing her amazedly. "Tell me this, you monkey. How on earth did a chit of a thing like you handle that scarecrow?"

"He—was lying in the road and—and I just picked him up and—and pushed him in," Emerence said rather faintly.

He reached out a hand and took her arm. She flinched away from him but he paid no heed. He felt her biceps and then turned to the Head, astonishment in his face, "She's got the biceps of a female infant Hercules! I couldn't make out how a slip of a thing like this could handle that thing. It's a good weight, you know. If *this* is how they grow 'em in Australia——"

He stopped, for the Head had given him a look which reminded him that this was a court of justice. Inwardly, she was dying to laugh; but she managed to control her face and went back to her question.

"Why did you do it, Emerence? You have given Commander Christy and Griffiths a great deal of trouble. Apart from that, you surely know that when you are left alone like that we trust you to go on quietly with your work? Don't you like to be trusted like that? Or would you rather know that we trust you so little that we always have someone on the watch with you?"

Emerence made no reply. Her fair head was drooping and she was biting her lower lip hard in a desperate effort not to cry. If the Head had scolded, it would have been

147

easier; but this quiet reasoning was very much more effective in her present state.

"Now," the Head said at last, "you see you make it difficult for us. If *one* girl is so little to be trusted, how are we to know that there are others just as bad?"

"They aren't!" Emerence burst out.

"No? Are you sure?"

"Yes—they—they always w-work when—they're alone," Emerence replied unevenly.

"Then why should you be the only one? You are truthful in word, I know. I can trust you there. Why am I not to trust you to be honest in your actions?"

No reply. Emerence knew that once she spoke the tears must come and she was determined not to cry before these people.

But she had to deal with a more obstinate person than herself. Miss Annersley was determined to break down the barrier, for she felt that once the child had given way, it would be possible to handle her and turn her into something more like the sort of girl the Chalet School prided itself on turning out.

"Why, Emerence?" she repeated.

Emerence made a last wild effort to control herself. Unfortunately for that, she glanced up and met the Head's eyes. What she saw in them struck home. She gulped once or twice, twisted her hands together fiercely and then, something gave way. She dropped on her knees at the Head's side, buried her head in her lap and wept long and loud.

A gesture from Miss Annersley cleared the room speedily. Rosalie escorted the Commander off the premises while Matron went off to San. to tuck a hot-water bottle into a bed and collect Emerence's pyjamas. She knew that after an outbreak like that only bed would be of use.

Meanwhile, the Head had stooped and lifted the thin little body on to her lap and then let Emerence cry herself quiet, which was not for some minutes, for there was a good deal to come and she had got well away. But when the loud sobs had grown less noisy and the heaving was not so violent, she began to talk.

What she said, Emerence never told anyone; but she never forgot it. By the time it ended, she understood as never before just why we can't do everything *we* like.

At last, with a hiccough she said, "But Mum and Dad let me."

"When you are tiny, people often do let you," Miss Annersley said quickly. It was no part of her policy to blame the Hopes to their child. "You are growing up now, and must learn to think of consequences when you do foolish things."

Emerence said no more. Then the Head pronounced her punishment. Her part in the Christmas play would be taken from her and given to someone else. That hurt, for Emerence had been very proud of having a speaking part, but she accepted it meekly. Then she was to go to Matron who would put her to bed in San. for the rest of the day. She would be alone there until next day and only Matron or the Head herself would go near her.

Emerence scrubbed her eyes with Miss Annersley's handkerchief—her own had given out long ago. Then she stumbled off the Head's lap.

"I—I'm sorry," she said with a gulp. "I—I see and I—I w-will t-try to be better."

"And that is all we ask of you," the Head said. "Now come to Matron. I will come up before Abendessen and see you again."

She left Emerence with Matron, who saw her to bed in strict silence and then left her to think of her sins. Not that *that* lasted long. What with one thing and another, the child was tired out and when Matron peeped in an hour later, she was fast asleep.

"Poor little soul!" murmured Matey, coming to tuck her up more closely. "Ah well, this is likely the turning-point. We've dealt with other problem children before and made something of them and I don't suppose there'll be much more trouble after this." She left the room and went off to one of the many duties awaiting her.

Emerence slept on through the whole afternoon and well on into the evening. In fact, it was nearly seven before she awoke and then it was only because the door squeaked loudly as it opened. She turned over and saw the Head and, of all people, Mary-Lou!

"Awake?" the Head said cheerily. "Matron will bring you a tray presently and Mary-Lou has something to say to you. Ten minutes, Mary-Lou, and no longer. Come straight to me then."

She turned away and left the two together, smiling broadly to herself as she went downstairs, for the interview with Mary-Lou had been on the funny side. She had told the girls what had happened and then had added that evidently there must have been trouble between them and Emerence, or the latter would not have been so silly. She suggested that it would be as well to wipe out old scores and begin again when the little Australian came back into school.

As the netball team had covered itself with glory, winning the match by nine-three, Julie for one was quite willing to accept this, and the rest of the prefects were ready to follow her lead.

"Besides," Bride ended for them, "we've plenty to worry about without fussing over a little ass like that. And, you know, it really was an awfully cute thing to rig up, though I wouldn't let her or any of the rest of the silly little idiots hear me."

"I should hope not!" Loveday said crushingly.

But the Head's words had set Mary-Lou's conscience going, the result being that she had tapped at the study door and asked to be allowed to see Emerence as she felt that most of the row was mainly *her* fault and she wanted to say she was sorry.

"What did Emerence do to upset you?" the Head asked.

"Oh, she just said—things."

Miss Annersley was wise enough to ask no more questions. She took Mary-Lou upstairs and went away to chuckle to herself over the young girl's insouciance.

"I've come to say I'm sorry for my share of it all," she said. "You've been an awful little owl, but we'll say no more about it."

"Well, I'm sorry I swore at you," Emerence got out.

150

sitting up and holding out her hand. "Shake, will you?"

They shook hands and then Mary-Lou glanced at the clock. "I've got about seven minutes left. You buck up and tell me how you really did stop up the over-flow. The Abbess only told us you had and I want to know how you managed it."

Thus urged, Emerence told, and Mary-Lou finally left the room gurgling over it. She had promised not to tell the others, but she meant to write about it to "Auntie Jo" who would certainly appreciate the story (*N.B.*—she did; and later used it as an incident in one of her own school stories!), and she had a dim kind of feeling that Emerence would more or less toe the line in future. At any rate, she wasn't likely to *swear* at any of them again! Mary-Lou skipped gaily downstairs without looking where she was going and wound up by jumping the last four and landing on top of the Head Girl, who speedily reduced her complacency by an order mark and a sharp scolding.

CHAPTER XVIII

"THE THREE KINGS"

"MARY-LOU, come here and let me see if those wings of yours are safe!"

"Lesley, I think I should pull your crown a tiny bit further forward. It's rather too far on the back of your head."

"*Girls—girls!* Not so much noise! You'll be heard right out in front! Aren't you nearly ready? It's almost time for the curtain to go up."

"Just ready, Miss Stephens," said Loveday, coming forward in her flowing robes of the Madonna. "How much longer?"

Miss Stephens, who was producing the Christmas play this year, glanced at her watch. "Just three minutes. The hall's full and I'm just going to tell them to lower the house-lights. Baby angels, are you in your lines? Then follow me and take your places. The rest of you be ready. And remember if you really *do* need the prompter, Miss Dene is sitting on the left-hand side of the stage and will be ready for you. I must go! Play up, all of you!"

She vanished, followed by a string of Juniors from St. Agnes' who were the "baby angels." Verity-Anne went with them. She had to open the play with a carol, for she owned a lark-like voice which was always an asset on these occasions.

The rest of the actors fell silent. It was a point of honour in the school that no noise should ever come from back-stage, once the house-lights were down. In front, the footlights sprang up and the baby angels ran to take their places while the tiny orchestra, made up of piano, fiddle, 'cello, flute and glockenspiel, struck up the gay music of "I Saw Three Ships."

The curtains parted and an angel slipped through. Her great white wings towered over her head on which was fixed a glimmering golden halo. A low murmur of admiration rose from the packed audience as they saw Verity-Anne, looking her most heavenly as she stood with arms spread wide. Then she opened her mouth and the merry carol rang out in sweet, birdlike notes:

> "I saw three ships come sailing in,
> Come sailing in, come sailing in.
> I saw three ships come sailing in
> On Christemas Day in the morning."

Behind the curtain, the baby angels joined in the last line, but Verity-Anne went on alone with the next verse. The effect of the very young voices was charming and the tinies had been well drilled. It went on like this until the soloist came to the verse beginning:

> "And all the bells on earth shall ring
> On Christemas Day, on Christemas Day,
> And all the bells on earth shall ring
> On Christemas Day in the morning."

As the glockenspiel, played by Herr Laubach, joined merrily in, the curtains were swung apart to show the baby angels dancing round in rings in time to the music, while greater angels came thronging to the sides. The scenery was merely curtains of midnight blue and the effect was of an illumination.

As the last words of the carol died away, the notes of the glockenspiel followed. Then a big angel in short tunic, golden sandals and many-hued wings gently pushed his way through the laughing baby angels and called, "Michael! Is all in readiness?" Another, bearing shield and sword joined him, saying, "Yea; all! The world awaits the coming told by you, oh Gabriel. Already the great star which shall call the Gentiles to worship shines in the East and men are hastening from distant lands—men who are earthly kings, coming to bow the knee and make offerings to the King of Heaven."

At once the music rang out again, this time in Peter Cornelius'· Christmas song, "Three Kings from Persian lands afar," and the whole choir joined in the splendid chorale. As it ended, the curtain fell and the audience remained silent. There was never any applause permitted at these Nativity plays which were traditional in the Chalet School.

When the stage was visible again, it was empty, but from behind the scenes, came a voice, singing the carol, "Now every child that dwells on earth." In the left-hand corner, a bright light shone down and as the carol ended, a small boy—Maeve Bettany—ran in, shielding her eyes and looking up at the light. She wore a brief tunic and carried a crook and was followed by two or three others. They clustered together, looking up and talking about the great star that had appeared so suddenly, wondering why it had come and what it meant. To them entered an Old King with a golden crown on his long white hair. His scarlet robes gleamed with many-coloured glass beads and he was a magnificent sight. Nancy Chester moved steadily forward to the group of boys who turned to stare at him and ask why they were gazing upwards. They pointed to the Star and told him how it had suddenly appeared in the sky from nowhere and everyone was wondering what it meant.

He told them that it meant that the King of all the World had been born to rule over the world.

"But that's God," Maeve said, her clear little voice reaching the farthest end of the big hall.

"Then God has been born," the Old King said.

The boys could not understand this. God had always been there. How could He be born?

As if in answer, an Eastern musician came strolling in, twanging a small harp and singing the old Flemish carol: "A little Child on earth has been born." The puzzled boys shook their heads. It was beyond their understanding. Presently a strange, unearthly sound rang out and one of them cried that it was supper-time. They must go. Laughing and calling, they ran out. The musician followed and the Old King was left alone.

Almost immediately, the Archangel Gabriel appeared with his hands full of lilies. He stood still in the light from the Star and the Old King approached him and bowing low asked if he was on the right path and if yonder Star were the one for which he looked.

The archangel told them that it was the sign sent from God that the Eastern King had been born. Even now, other kings were on the way to bow to Him and to make Him their offerings. The Old King must wait and they would come and then all would go forward together.

"How do I know that this is naught but a dream?" the Old King asked. "Old men dream many dreams. Are you not one of them?"

The archangel gave him a lily-spray. "Dreams leave no living flowers behind them," he said. "Take this as surety from the garden of Paradise. And for the rest—harken!"

Then the old fourteenth-century carol, "Angelus ad Virginem," rang out over the hushed, listening audience with something of unearthliness in it. The curtains fell on the end of the carol, to rise again almost at once, showing the Old King with his servants clustered round him listening, as the orchestra played pianissimo the air of Gabriel's song. Then there came a clanking and a magnificent warrior, in surcoat of white and gold over a

154

tunic of green, stalked in. The field of his shield was green with a golden lily traced on it and his crown of green and gold was set round a gilded helmet. Primrose held her head rather stiffly, for the cardboard helmet was none too steady and they had found no means of securing it to her hair. But she looked every inch a warrior king as she greeted the Old King who represented Wisdom and told of her pilgrimage to seek the King of the World.

The Old King told of Gabriel's visit to him and pointed to the Star. He said that the archangel had told him other kings were coming to do homage to the Child, too. They had best wait. He was weary and would slumber awhile.

"But I am not weary," the warrior said. "Do you sleep and I will keep guard, for it is meet that those in the prime of life should guard and cherish the old that cared for them when they were small and needed care. Rest, oh brother! Be at peace. I will keep watch."

The Old King lay down, his followers clustering round him while the warrior stood to attention. All lights except the light from the Star were dimmed and as the Old King slept, the baby angels ran softly in, singing the German carol, "O Jesulein süss, O Jesulein mild" (Oh wee Jesus sweet, Oh wee Jesus mild). The curtains fell again and when they rose, the angels were gone and a black king stood by, his head covered with the head-dress still worn by the Arabs of the desert and a plain band holding it in place. The Young King—a negro, as tradition always gives us.

Humbly he came forward to greet his brothers who hailed him as one of themselves. They talked together. The Old King pointed to the Star and told of Gabriel's message. The Warrior King asked if any more would come, but the others could not say. Then Michael appeared and bade them set out, for they were the vanguard of an army of kings who would follow during time to pay homage to the great King of the World.

The Three Kings prepared to set forth on their journey and Michael, mingling with the servants of the Old King, vanished. The orchestra played the melancholy sweetness of the carol, "We Three Kings of Orient are," and the

155

Three Kings sang it amongst them, the servants on the stage and the rest behind the scenes singing the chorus and the last verse with them. The curtains fell once more and the angels all crowded before them, singing, "How brightly gleams the morning Star" first and then the French carol, "Le vermeil du soleil." The lights went out as they finished, but flashed up again in one minute, by which time not an angel was to be seen. The curtains parted to show Herod's palace and Herod himself seated on a throne at the head of the table.

Tom Gay had been chosen for Herod, and, with her amazing height, she looked the part down to the ground. Rosalie Way was Queen Elpis, sitting at his side. A murmur of talk rose from the courtiers which was broken by the entrance of a small page-boy who ran in excitedly. This was the part Emerence should have played and behind the scenes, clad as a shepherd, she was wishing heartily that she had not tried to do anything so silly as dam the overflow of the pond. However, it was too late now. Anyhow, she was friends again with her form and Mary-Lou was standing by her, so things might have been much worse. Despite her disappointment, Emerence was a much happier girl now than she had been before and she joined in the carols with all her might.

The part had, in the end, been given to Angela Carter. She went up to the throne and knelt before Herod who asked what news she brought.

"Oh King, live for ever!" Angela squeaked, rising two or three tones higher than usual. "Three monarchs are at the gate."

"Three monarchs! We know naught of any such coming to us," Herod said, frowning severely on Angela to make her pull herself together.

She succeeded, for Angela's next lines came in her own natural tones. "My lord, they say they are come to seek for the King that shall be born and have followed His Star many long miles. And they are great kings without a doubt, for they ride on white camels and are all agleam with precious stones."

156

"Bid them enter," Herod said sharply. "My Queen, you and your ladies have our leave to depart."

Elpis rose, bowed low to Herod and made a stately exit, followed by her ladies. The page went after them and returned, leading the Three Kings.

For this scene, Madge had kept closely to the story given in St. Matthew. Herod's question was answered by the Kings in unison and the soothsayers and the Temple priests spoke the Old Testament prophecies. Finally, Herod bade the Kings go and seek the Baby King, and when they had found Him, return with the news, that he too might go and adore. The Three Kings agreed that unless anything hindered they would bring back the news. Then they went out, led by the page, and the curtain fell on Herod's fury. At once the choir struck up the very old traditional carol, "King Herod and the Cock," following it with "God Rest you Merry, Gentlemen." Then the curtains were drawn to show the first of the stable scenes. In the centre was a wooden trough filled with straw in which lay the Bambino. The Madonna sat at the head, one arm stretched along the side of the trough, her head bent over the Bambino. St. Joseph knelt at the other end and all round stood the angels and archangels with bowed heads. There was no singing to this tableau, but the orchestra played the Pastoral symphony from "The Messiah" and the audience were very still as they watched "The Adoration of Heaven."

When the curtains fell, there was a low sigh of regret. The tableau was beautiful and the faces of the girls showed such understanding and reverence that it was strangely impressive.

Then Madge's sweet mezzo sounded in the French carol, "Dans cette étable," and was followed by Verity-Anne in the quaint old Cuckoo Carol. Both sang just behind the curtains and this added to the unearthliness of it.

The stage was empty save for the trough, the Madonna and St. Joseph when the curtains were swept back again and, still leaning over the trough, her eyes on the

157

Bambino's face, Loveday sang, in a deep contralto that no one had realised she had, the beloved carol, "Stille Nacht, Heilige Nacht." Her voice was of no great power, but the notes were rich and yet clear and with a sweetness in them that rivalled Madge's. As she ended, Gabriel entered leading the shepherds, who knelt to offer their crooks and hurriedly-made rustic toys. The Madonna, still bending, raised her hand gently to acknowledge the gifts and Gabriel led his charges to the side. The wandering musician came next with his harp and accompanying him were the boys with their offerings. A group of little girls brought bands of linen and woollen baby clothes which would be sent to the London Mission to which the school subscribed. They were all in the charge of Raphael, who came at the call of Gabriel. He in his turn called St. Michael, who led in the Three Kings with their rich gifts of gold, frankincense and myrrh. Then the angels came, the baby angels, linked by a long chain of daisies which they carried in their hands and on their shoulders, and the other angels with handfuls of flowers which they laid beside the other gifts. As each group offered its gifts, it turned to the side till presently the whole of the back and sides of the stage were filled. The humans stood to the front, each in charge of their own archangel. The baby angels stood in a smiling band in front of them and, at the back, tier on tier of the great angels stood with clasped hands and lifted heads. One great chord came from the orchestra and the whole school sang with full-voiced invitation, that loveliest of Latin hymns—"Adeste Fideles."

When the hymn ended, the curtains fell but rose again a moment later to show the Madonna standing holding up the Bambino for all to see, while all the humans were kneeling, holding out longing hands to "the Babe Who is Lord of All." The orchestra broke into the old triumphant air of "All hail, the power of Jesu's Name," and to its strains the curtain fell for the last time. The Christmas play was over.

"Why did I feel like crying?" Emerence asked wonderingly of Julie Lucy who happened to pass her at the moment.

Julie stopped. "Because we did it *meaning* it—every word of it," she said gravely.

"And because it is the truest and loveliest story in all the world," added a new voice, one that Emerence had never heard before.

The rest knew it, though, and gathered round its owner with stifled cries of delight, demanding to know where she had sprung from.

"Oh," said Joey Maynard, beaming at them over the two tiny babies she held hugged in her arms. "I just *couldn't* let the school have a Christmas play and me not there to see it. Jack had to come on business and my sister said she'd look after the rest of the family, so I decided to fly with him and bring my twins to show off *and*," this with great emphasis, "to top off the end of the term with a real shock for the Chalet School!"

CAPTAIN ARMADA

has a whole shipload of exciting books for you

Armadas are chosen by children all over the world. They're designed to fit your pocket, and your pocket money too. They're colourful, exciting, and there are hundreds of titles to choose from. Armada has something for everyone:

Mystery and adventure series to collect, with favourite characters and authors . . . like Alfred Hitchcock and The Three Investigators – The Hardy Boys – young detective Nancy Drew – the intrepid Lone Piners – Biggles – the rascally William – and others.

Hair-raising Spinechillers – Ghost, Monster and Science Fiction stories. Fascinating quiz and puzzle books. Exciting hobby books. Lots of hilarious fun books. Many famous stories. Thrilling pony adventures. Popular school stories – and many more.

You can build up your own Armada collection – and new Armadas are published every month, so look out for the latest additions to the Captain's cargo.

Armadas are available in bookshops and newsagents.

Armada